David Munro

Lyrical poetry for boys and girls

David Munro

Lyrical poetry for boys and girls

ISBN/EAN: 9783742842688

Manufactured in Europe, USA, Canada, Australia, Japa

Cover: Foto ©Andreas Hilbeck / pixelio.de

Manufactured and distributed by brebook publishing software
(www.brebook.com)

David Munro

Lyrical poetry for boys and girls

LYRICAL POETRY

FOR BOYS AND GIRLS.

SELECTED AND ARRANGED BY

DAVID MUNRO.

LONDON: GEORGE BELL & SONS, YORK STREET,
COVENT GARDEN.
1891.

PREFACE.

DURING more than twenty years' experience as a school-master, I have proved the superiority of Lyrical Poetry over any other form of verse for those exercises in learning by heart which form so important a part in the mental and moral training of youth.

For boys, especially, the Lyric—telling its single, and often stirring tale of Truth and Faith, of Danger and of Duty, in musical and measured rhythm—has a peculiar charm, but I know of no selection of Poetry for boys composed solely of Lyrics of this class.

I have spared no pains in collating each poem in the present volume with editions having the most authority, and I venture to hope that, in this respect, it may bear favourable comparison with most existing selections, many of which are marked by great inaccuracy, and a too great readiness to accept readings which are themselves perpetuations of previous errors.

The poetry of Sentiment has, as will be seen, been made subordinate to the poetry of Action, and the value of almost every piece, as a fit subject for repetition, has been tested by experience.

I desire to tender my grateful acknowledgments to Mrs. Craik, Mr. Browning, Messrs. Longmans, Macmillan, and others, for their kind permission to insert copyright poems which have greatly added to the value of the selection.

D. M.

HILLSIDE, ELSTREE,
October, 1880.

CONTENTS.

———

		PAGE
I Remember, I Remember	*T. Hood*	1
Ode to the Cuckoo	*J. Logan*	2
Rule, Britannia	*J. Thomson*	3
The Graves of a Household	*F. D. Hemans*	4
Song	*Sir W. Scott*	5
To-Day	*T. Carlyle*	6
The Scottish Exile's Farewell	*T. Pringle*	7
The Wild Gazelle	*Lord Byron*	8
To the Cuckoo	*W. Wordsworth*	8
The Character of a Happy Life	*Sir H. Wotton*	9
Coronach	*Sir W. Scott*	10
The Sea	*B. W. Procter*	11
Ho! Breakers on the Weather Bow	*C. Swain*	12
Men of England	*T. Campbell*	13
The Song of a Mariner	*A. Cunningham*	14
The Homes of England	*F. D. Hemans*	15
The Knight's Tomb	*S. T. Coleridge*	16
The Trumpet	*F. D. Hemans*	16
The Skylark	*T. Hogg*	17
The Destruction of Sennacherib	*Lord Byron*	18
A Psalm of Life	*H. W. Longfellow*	19
He never Smiled again	*F. D. Hemans*	20
Vision of Belshazzar	*Lord Byron*	21
Casabianca	*F. D. Hemans*	23

Contents.

		PAGE
BANNOCKBURN	R. Burns	24
NOW	... A. A. Procter	25
FLOWERS WITHOUT FRUIT	J. H. Newman	26
THE SOLDIER'S DREAM	... T. Campbell	26
THE BURIAL OF SIR JOHN MOORE	... C. Wolfe	27
MAXIMUS	... A. A. Procter	28
JUDGE NOT	A. A. Procter	30
THE LIGHT OF STARS	H W. Longfellow	30
THE FLIGHT OF XERXES	M. J. Jewsbury	32
ELIZABETH AT TILBURY	F. T. Palgrave	33
LOCHINVAR	Sir W. Scott	34
CRESCENTIUS	L. E. Landon	36
THE CURFEW SONG OF ENGLAND	F. D. Hemans	37
THE SICILIAN VESPERS	J. G. Whittier	39
ADIEU	T. Carlyle	41
A HIGHLAND BOAT SONG	... Sir W. Scott	42
DOWN ON THE SHORE	W. Allingham	43
"SPEAK KINDLY"	... Woodman	44
BE STRONG	A. A. Procter	45
SONG FOR AUGUST	H. Martineau	46
THE ROVER	Sir W. Scott	47
ALONG THE SHORE	... D. M. Craik	47
THE BUILDERS	... H. W. Longfellow	48
THE BATTLE OF MORGARTEN	F. D. Hemans	49
SATURDAY AFTERNOON	N. P. Willis	52
THE FROST SPIRIT	J. G. Whittier	53
ONE BY ONE	A. A. Procter	55
THE BATTLE OF HOHENLINDEN ...	... T. Campbell	⁻56
YE MARINERS OF ENGLAND	T. Campbell	57
BERNARDO AND ALPHONSO	J. G. Lockhart	58
VICTOR GALBRAITH	... H. W. Longfellow	60
THE BURIAL OF THE CHAMPION OF HIS CLASS, AT YALE COLLEGE	... N. P. Willis	62
BOADICEA	W. Cowper	63
THE SEA FIGHT	... B. W Procter	65

Contents.

PAGE

GELERT'S GRAVE ...   W. R. Spencer 66

EXCELSIOR ...   H. W. Longfellow 70

THE BENDED BOW   F. D. Hemans 71

THE FUGITIVES ...   ... P. B. Shelley 73

ON A DISTANT PROSPECT OF ETON COLLEGE T. Gray 75

WAR SONG   Sir W. Scott 78

THE LOSS OF THE ROYAL GEORGE ... W. Cowper 79

SIR NICHOLAS AT MARSTON MOOR ... W. M. Praed 81

THE INCHCAPE ROCK ...   ... R. Southey 83

ELEGY WRITTEN IN A COUNTRY CHURCHYARD ... T. Gray 85

LORD ULLIN'S DAUGHTER ... T. Campbell 89

THE CLOUD ...   ... P. B. Shelley 91

MY PSALM   J. G. Whittier 94

THE SPANISH ARMADA   Lord Macaulay 96

THE BATTLE AUTUMN OF 1862 J. G. Whittier 100

THE VILLAGE BLACKSMITH H. W. Longfellow 101

THE BELLS   E. A. Poe 103

TO A SKYLARK   ... P. B. Shelley 106

DEATH'S FINAL CONQUEST ... J. Shirley 109

HOW THEY BROUGHT THE GOOD NEWS FROM GHENT TO AIX

       R. Browning 110

THE BATTLE OF BLENHEIM ... R. Southey 112

THE ENGLISH BOY   F. D. Hemans 114

IVRY   Lord Macaulay 116

BATTLE OF THE BALTIC ... T. Campbell 119

BALLAD OF ROSABELLE   ... Sir W. Scott 121

THE PIPES AT LUCKNOW ... J. G. Whittier 123

THE LADDER OF ST. AUGUSTINE H. W. Longfellow 125

THE DIVERTING HISTORY OF JOHN GILPIN W. Cowper 127

THE BALLAD OF CHEVY CHASE ...   135

THE DREAM OF EUGENE ARAM T. Hood 141

MY LOST YOUTH   ... H. W. Longfellow 147

LYRICAL POETRY
FOR BOYS AND GIRLS.

I REMEMBER, I REMEMBER.

I REMEMBER, I remember,
The house where I was born,
The little window where the sun
Came peeping in at morn;
He never came a wink too soon,
Nor brought too long a day,
But now, I often wish the night
Had borne my breath away!

I remember, I remember,
The roses, red and white,
The violets, and the lily-cups,
Those flowers made of light!
The lilacs where the robin built,
And where my brother set
The laburnum on his birth-day,—
The tree is living yet!

I remember, I remember
Where I was used to swing,
And thought the air must rush as fresh
To swallows on the wing;
My spirit flew in feathers then,
That is so heavy now,
And summer pools could hardly cool
The fever on my brow!

B

I remember, I remember
The fir trees dark and high ;
I used to think their slender tops
Were close against the sky :
It was a childish ignorance,
But now 'tis little joy
To know I'm farther off from heav'n
Than when I was a boy.

T. HOOD.

ODE TO THE CUCKOO.

HAIL, beauteous stranger of the grove !
  Thou messenger of spring !
Now Heaven repairs thy rural seat,
  And woods thy welcome sing.

What time the daisy decks the green,
  Thy certain voice we hear ;
Hast thou a star to guide thy path,
  Or mark the rolling year ?

Delightful visitant ! with thee
  I hail the time of flowers,
And hear the sound of music sweet
  From birds among the bowers.

The school-boy, wandering through the wood
  To pull the primrose gay,
Starts, the new voice of Spring to hear,
  And imitates thy lay.

What time the pea puts on the bloom
  Thou fliest thy vocal vale,
An annual guest in other lands,
  Another Spring to hail.

Sweet bird! thy bower is ever green,
  Thy sky is ever clear;
Thou hast no sorrow in thy song,
  No winter in thy year!

O, could I fly, I'd fly with thee!
  We'd make, with joyful wing,
Our annual visit o'er the globe,
  Companions of the spring.

J. Logan.

RULE, BRITANNIA.

When Britain first, at Heaven's command,
  Arose from out the azure main,
This was the charter of the land,
  And guardian angels sung this strain:
  " Rule, Britannia, rule the waves;
  Britons never will be slaves."

The nations, not so bless'd as thee,
  Must, in their turns, to tyrants fall;
While thou shalt flourish great and free,
  The dread and envy of them all.

Still more majestic shalt thou rise,
  More dreadful from each foreign stroke;
As the loud blast that tears the skies
  Serves but to root thy native oak.

Thee haughty tyrants ne'er shall tame;
  All their attempts to bend thee down
Will but arouse thy generous flame,
  But work their woe, and thy renown.

To thee belongs the rural reign;
  Thy cities shall with commerce shine;
All thine shall be the subject main;
  And every shore it circles, thine.

The Muses, still with freedom found,
  Shall to thy happy coast repair:
Bless'd isle! with matchless beauty crown'd,
  And manly hearts to guard the fair:
    " Rule, Britannia, rule the waves,
    Britons never will be slaves."

                                        J. Thomson.

THE GRAVES OF A HOUSEHOLD.

They grew in beauty side by side,
  They filled one home with glee ;—
Their graves are severed far and wide,
  By mount, and stream, and sea.

The same fond mother bent at night
  O'er each fair sleeping brow :
She had each folded flower in sight—
  Where are those dreamers now ?

One, 'midst the forests of the West,
  By a dark stream is laid—
The Indian knows his place of rest,
  Far in the cedar-shade.

The sea, the blue lone sea, hath one—
  He lies where pearls lie deep ;
He was the loved of all, yet none
  O'er his low bed may weep.

One sleeps where Southern vines are drest
  Above the noble slain :
He wrapt his colours round his breast
  On a blood-red field of Spain.

And one—o'er *her* the myrtle showers
  Its leaves, by soft winds fanned ;
She faded 'midst Italian flowers —
  The last of that bright band.

And parted thus they rest, who played
　　Beneath the same green tree ;
Whose voices mingled as they prayed
　　Around one parent knee ;

They that with smiles lit up the hall,
　　And cheered with song the hearth !—
Alas for love ! if *thou* wert all,
　　And naught beyond, O Earth !

F. D. HEMANS.

SONG.

" SOLDIER, rest ! thy warfare o'er,
　　Sleep the sleep that knows not breaking ;
Dream of battled fields no more,
　　Days of danger, nights of waking.
In our isle's enchanted hall,
　　Hands unseen thy couch are strewing,
Fairy strains of music fall,
　　Every sense in slumber dewing.
Soldier, rest ! thy warfare o'er,
Dream of fighting-fields no more :
Sleep the sleep that knows not breaking,
Morn of toil, nor night of waking.

" No rude sound shall reach thine ear,
　　Armour's clang, or war-steed champing,
Trump nor pibroch summon here
　　Mustering clan, or squadron tramping.
Yet the lark's shrill fife may come
　　At the day-break from the fallow,
And the bittern sound his drum,
　　Booming from the sedgy shallow.
Ruder sounds shall none be near,
Guards nor warders challenge here,
Here's no war-steed's neigh and champing,
Shouting clans or squadrons stamping.

"Huntsman, rest! thy chase is done,
 While our slumbrous spells assail ye,
Dream not, with the rising sun,
 Bugles here shall sound reveillé.
Sleep! the deer is in his den;
 Sleep! thy hounds are by thee lying;
Sleep! nor dream in yonder glen,
 How thy gallant steed lay dying.
Huntsman, rest! thy chase is done,
Think not of the rising sun,
For at dawning to assail ye,
Here no bugles sound reveillé."

SIR W. SCOTT.

TO-DAY.

So here hath been dawning
 Another blue Day:
Think wilt thou let it
 Slip useless away.

Out of Eternity
 This new Day is born;
Into Eternity,
 At night, will return.

Behold it aforetime
 No eye ever did:
So soon it for ever
 From all eyes is hid.

Here hath been dawning
 Another blue Day:
Think wilt thou let it
 Slip useless away.

T. CARLYLE.

THE SCOTTISH EXILE'S FAREWELL.

Our native Land—our native Vale—
    A long and last adieu !
Farewell to bonny Lynden-dale,
    And Cheviot-mountains blue !

Farewell, ye hills of glorious deeds,
    And streams renowned in song ;
Farewell, ye blithesome braes and meads
    Our hearts have loved so long.

Farewell, ye broomy elfin knowes,
    Where thyme and harebells grow ;
Farewell, ye hoary haunted howes,
    O'erhung with birk and sloe.

The battle-mound, the Border-tower,
    That Scotia's annals tell ;
The martyr's grave, the lover's bower —
    To each—to all—farewell !

Home of our hearts ! our fathers' home !
    Land of the brave and free !
The sail is flashing through the foam
    That bears us far from thee :

We seek a wild and distant shore,
    Beyond the Atlantic main ;
We leave thee to return no more,
    Nor view thy cliffs again :

But may dishonour blight our fame,
    And quench our household fires.
When we, or ours, forget thy name,
    Green Island of our Sires !

Our native Land—our native Vale—
    A long, a last adieu !
Farewell to bonny Lynden-dale,
    And Scotland's mountains blue !

T. Pringle.

THE WILD GAZELLE.

THE wild gazelle on Judah's hills
 Exulting yet may bound,
And drink from all the living rills
 That gush on holy ground:
Its airy step and glorious eye
May glance in tameless transport by :—

A step as fleet, an eye more bright,
 Hath Judah witness'd there;
And o'er her scenes of lost delight,
 Inhabitants more fair.
The cedars wave on Lebanon,
But Judah's statelier maids are gone!

More blest each palm that shades those plains
 Than Israel's scatter'd race;
For, taking root, it there remains
 In solitary grace:
It cannot quit its place of birth,
It will not live in other earth.

But we must wander witheringly,
 In other lands to die;
And where our fathers' ashes be,
 Our own may never lie:
Our temple hath not left a stone,
And Mockery sits on Salem's throne.

LORD BYRON.

TO THE CUCKOO.

O BLITHE new-comer! I have heard,
I hear thee and rejoice:
O Cuckoo! shall I call thee bird,
Or but a wandering voice?

While I am lying on the grass,
Thy loud note smites my ear!
From hill to hill it seems to pass,
At once far off and near!

I hear thee babbling to the vale
Of sunshine and of flowers;
And unto me thou bring'st a tale
Of visionary hours.

Thrice welcome, darling of the Spring!
Even yet thou art to me
No bird; but an invisible thing,
A voice, a mystery.

The same whom in my school-boy days
I listened to; that cry
Which made me look a thousand ways
In bush, and tree, and sky.

To seek thee did I often rove
Through woods and on the green;
And thou wert still a hope, a love;
Still longed for, never seen!

And I can listen to thee yet;
Can lie upon the plain
And listen, till I do beget
That golden time again.

O blessed bird! the earth we pace
Again appears to be
An unsubstantial, fairy place;
That is fit home for thee!

W. WORDSWORTH.

THE CHARACTER OF A HAPPY LIFE.

How happy is he born and taught,
    That serveth not another's will:
Whose armour is his honest thought,
    And simple truth his utmost skill;

Whose passions not his masters are;
    Whose soul is still prepared for death,
Untied unto the world by care
    Of public fame or private breath;

Who envies none that chance doth raise,
  Or vice; who never understood
How deepest wounds are given by praise;
  Nor rules of state, but rules of good;

Who hath his life from humours freed;
  Whose conscience is his strong retreat;
Whose state can neither flatterers feed,
  Nor ruin make accusers great;

Who God doth late and early pray
  More of His grace than gifts to lend;
And entertains the harmless day
  With a religious book or friend.

This man is freed from servile bands
  Of hope to rise or fear to fall:
Lord of himself, though not of lands,
  And, having nothing, yet hath all.
                    SIR H. WOTTON.

CORONACH.

HE is gone on the mountain,
  He is lost to the forest,
Like a summer-dried fountain,
  When our need was the sorest.
The font, reappearing,
  From the rain-drops shall borrow,
But to us comes no cheering,
  To Duncan no morrow!

The hand of the reaper
  Takes the ears that are hoary,
But the voice of the weeper
  Wails manhood in glory.
The autumn winds rushing
  Waft the leaves that are searest,
But our flower was in flushing,
  When blighting was nearest.

Fleet foot on the correi,
 Sage counsel in cumber,
Red hand in the foray,
 How sound is thy slumber!
Like the dew on the mountain,
 Like the foam on the river,
Like the bubble on the fountain,
 Thou art gone, and for ever!

SIR W. SCOTT.

THE SEA.

THE Sea! the Sea! the open Sea!
The blue, the fresh, the ever free!
Without a mark, without a bound,
It runneth the earth's wide regions 'round;
It plays with the clouds; it mocks the skies;
Or like a cradled creature lies.

I'm on the Sea! I'm on the Sea!
I am where I would ever be;
With the blue above, and the blue below,
And silence wheresoe'er I go;
If a storm should come and awake the deep,
What matter?   *I* shall ride and sleep.

I love (oh! *how* I love) to ride
On the fierce foaming bursting tide,
When every mad wave drowns the moon,
Or whistles aloft his tempest tune,
And tells how goeth the worlds below,
And why the south-west blasts do blow.

I never was on the dull tame shore,
But I loved the great Sea more and more,
And backwards flew to her billowy breast,
Like a bird that seeketh its mother's nest;
And a mother she *was*, and *is* to me;
For I was born on the open Sea!

The waves were white, and red the morn,
In the noisy hour when I was born;
And the whale it whistled, the porpoise rolled,
And the dolphins bared their backs of gold;
And never was heard such an outcry wild
As welcomed to life the Ocean-child!

I've lived since then, in calm and strife,
Full fifty summers a sailor's life,
With wealth to spend and a power to range,
But never have sought, or sighed for change;
And Death whenever he comes to me,
Shall come on the wild unbounded Sea!

B. W. PROCTER.

HO! BREAKERS ON THE WEATHER BOW.

Ho! breakers on the weather bow,
    And hissing white the sea;
Go, loose the topsail, mariner,
    And set the helm a-lee:
And set the helm a-lee, my boys,
    And shift her while ye may;
Or not a living soul on board
    Will view the light of day.

Aloft the seaman daringly
    Shook out the rattling sail;
The danger fled—she leapt a-head
    Like wild stag through the gale:
Like wild stag through the gale, my boys,
    All panting as in fear,
And trembling as her spirit knew
    Destruction in the rear!

Now slacken speed—take weary heed—
    All hands haul home the sheet;
To Him who saves, amidst the waves,
    Let each their prayer repeat:

Let each their prayer repeat, my boys,
    For but a moment's gain
Lay 'tween our breath and instant death
    Within that howling main.

                C. SWAIN.

MEN OF ENGLAND.

MEN of England! who inherit
    Rights that cost your sires their blood!
Men whose undegenerate spirit
    Has been proved on land and flood :—

By the foes ye've fought uncounted,
    By the glorious deeds ye've done,
Trophies captured—breaches mounted,
    Navies conquer'd—kingdoms won!

Yet, remember, England gathers
    Hence but fruitless wreaths of fame,
If the patriotism of your fathers
    Glow not in your hearts the same.

What are monuments of bravery,
    Where no public virtues bloom?
What avail in lands of slavery,
    Trophied temples, arch and tomb?

Pageants!—let the world revere us
    For our people's rights and laws,
And the breasts of civic heroes
    Bared in Freedom's holy cause.

Yours are Hampden's, Russell's glory,
    Sydney's matchless shade is yours,—
Martyrs in heroic story,
    Worth a hundred Agincourts!

We're the sons of sires that baffled
  Crown'd and mitred tyranny :—
They defied the field and scaffold
  For their birthrights—so will we !
                                          T. CAMPBELL.

———·———

THE SONG OF A MARINER.

A WET sheet and a flowing sea,
  A wind that follows fast,
And fills the white and rustling sail,
  And bends the gallant mast ;
And bends the gallant mast, my boys,
  While, like the eagle free,
Away the good ship flies, and leaves
  Old England on the lee.

O for a soft and gentle wind !
  I heard a fair one cry ;
But give to me the snoring breeze,
  And white waves heaving high ;
And white waves heaving high, my boys,
  The good ship tight and free—
The world of waters is our home,
  And merry men are we.

There's tempest in yon hornèd moon,
  And lightning in yon cloud ;
And hark the music, mariners !
  The wind is piping loud ;
The wind is piping loud, my boys,
  The lightning flashing free—
While the hollow oak our palace is,
  Our heritage the sea.
                                          A. CUNNINGHAM.

THE HOMES OF ENGLAND.

THE stately homes of England!
　How beautiful they stand,
Amidst their tall ancestral trees,
　O'er all the pleasant land!
The deer across their greensward bound,
　Through shade and sunny gleam;
And the swan glides past them with the sound
　Of some rejoicing stream.

The merry homes of England!
　Around their hearths by night,
What gladsome looks of household love
　Meet in the ruddy light!
There woman's voice flows forth in song,
　Or childhood's tale is told,
Or lips move tunefully along
　Some glorious page of old.

The blessed homes of England!
　How swiftly on their bowers
Is laid the holy quietness
　That breathes from Sabbath hours!
Solemn, yet sweet, the church-bell's chime
　Floats through their woods at morn;
All other sounds, in that still time,
　Of breeze and leaf are born.

The cottage homes of England!
　By thousands on her plains
They are smiling o'er the silvery brooks,
　And round the hamlet fanes.
Through glowing orchards forth they peep,
　Each from its nook of leaves;
And fearless there the lowly sleep,
　As the bird beneath their eaves.

The free, fair homes of England!
　Long, long, in hut and hall,
May hearts of native proof be reared
　To guard each hallowed wall!
And green for ever be the groves,
　And bright the flowery sod,
Where first the child's glad spirit loves
　Its country and its God!

F. D. HEMANS.

THE KNIGHT'S TOMB.

WHERE is the grave of Sir Arthur O'Kellyn?
　Where may the grave of that good man be?—
By the side of a spring, on the breast of Helvellyn,
　Under the twigs of a young birch tree!
The oak that in summer was sweet to hear,
And rustled its leaves in the fall of the year,
And whistled and roared in the winter alone,
Is gone,—and the birch in its stead is grown.—
　The Knight's bones are dust,
　And his good sword rust;—
His soul is with the saints, I trust.

S. T. COLERIDGE.

THE TRUMPET.

THE trumpet's voice hath roused the land—
　Light up the beacon pyre!
A hundred hills have seen the brand,
　And waved the sign of fire.
A hundred banners to the breeze
　Their gorgeous folds have cast—
And, hark! was that the sound of seas?
　A king to war went past.

The chief is arming in his hall,
　The peasant by his hearth;
The mourner hears the thrilling call,
　And rises from the earth.
The mother on her first-born son
　Looks with a boding eye—
They come not back, though all be won,
　Whose young hearts leap so high.

The bard hath ceased his song, and bound
　The falchion to his side;
Even for the marriage altar crowned
　The lover quits his bride.
And all this haste, and change, and fear,
　By earthly clarion spread!—
How will it be when kingdoms hear
　The blast that wakes the dead?

　　　　　　　　　F. D. HEMANS.

THE SKYLARK.

　BIRD of the wilderness,
　Blithesome and cumberless,
Sweet be thy matin o'er moorland and lea!
　Emblem of happiness,
　Blest is thy dwelling place,
Oh to abide in the desert with thee!

　Wild is thy lay and loud,
　Far in the downy cloud,
Love gives it energy, love gave it birth.
　Where, on thy dewy wing,
　Where art thou journeying?
Thy lay is in heaven, thy love is on earth.

　O'er fell and fountain sheen,
　O'er moor and mountain green,

　　　　　　　　　　　　　　C

O'er the red streamer that heralds the day,
 Over the cloudlet dim,
 Over the rainbow's rim,
Musical cherub, soar, singing away !

 Then, when the gloaming comes,
 Low in the heather blooms,
Sweet will thy welcome and bed of love be,
 Emblem of happiness,
 Blest is thy dwelling-place—
Oh to abide in the desert with thee!

T. HOGG.

THE DESTRUCTION OF SENNACHERIB.

THE Assyrian came down like the wolf on the fold,
And his cohorts were gleaming in purple and gold;
And the sheen of their spears was like stars on the sea,
When the blue wave rolls nightly on deep Galilee.

Like the leaves of the forest when Summer is green,
That host with their banners at sunset were seen:
Like the leaves of the forest when Autumn hath blown,
That host on the morrow lay wither'd and strown.

For the Angel of Death spread his wings on the blast,
And breathed in the face of the foe as he pass'd;
And the eyes of the sleepers wax'd deadly and chill,
And their hearts but once heav'd, and for ever grew still!

And there lay the steed with his nostril all wide,
But through it there roll'd not the breath of his pride:
And the foam of his gasping lay white on the turf,
And cold as the spray of the rock-beating surf.

And there lay the rider distorted and pale,
With the dew on his brow and the rust on his mail;
And the tents were all silent, the banners alone,
The lances unlifted, the trumpet unblown.

And the widows of Ashur are loud in their wail,
And the idols are broke in the temple of Baal;
And the might of the Gentile, unsmote by the sword,
Hath melted like snow in the glance of the Lord!

LORD BYRON.

A PSALM OF LIFE.

TELL me not, in mournful numbers,
  "Life is but an empty dream!"
For the soul is dead that slumbers,
  And things are not what they seem.

Life is real! Life is earnest!
  And the grave is not its goal;
"Dust thou art, to dust returnest,"
  Was not spoken of the soul.

Not enjoyment, and not sorrow,
  Is our destined end or way;
But to act, that each to-morrow
  Find us farther than to-day.

Art is long, and Time is fleeting,
  And our hearts, though stout and brave,
Still, like muffled drums, are beating
  Funeral marches to the grave.

In the world's broad field of battle,
  In the bivouac of Life,
Be not like dumb, driven cattle!
  Be a hero in the strife!

Trust no Future, howe'er pleasant!
  Let the dead Past bury its dead!
Act,—act in the living Present!
  Heart within, and God o'erhead!

Lives of great men all remind us
    We can make our lives sublime,
And, departing, leave behind us
    Footprints on the sands of time :—

Footprints, that perhaps another,
    Sailing o'er life's solemn main,
A forlorn and shipwrecked brother,
    Seeing, shall take heart again.

Let us, then, be up and doing,
    With a heart for any fate ;
Still achieving, still pursuing,
    Learn to labour and to wait.

                    H. W. LONGFELLOW.

HE NEVER SMILED AGAIN.

THE bark that held a prince went down,
    The sweeping waves rolled on ;
And what was England's glorious crown
    To him that wept a son ?
He lived—for life may long be borne
    Ere sorrow break its chain :
Why comes not death to those who mourn ?
    He never smiled again.

There stood proud forms before his throne,
    The stately and the brave ;
But which could fill the place of one,
    That one beneath the wave ?
Before him passed the young and fair,
    In pleasure's reckless train ;
But seas dashed o'er his son's bright hair—
    He never smiled again.

He sat where festal bowls went round,
. He heard the minstrel sing,
He saw the tourney's victor crowned
    Amidst the knightly ring:
A murmur of the restless deep
    Was blent with every strain,
A voice of winds that would not sleep—
    He never smiled again.

Hearts in that time closed o'er the trace
    Of vows once fondly poured,
And strangers took the kinsman's place
    At many a joyous board;
Graves, which true love had bathed with tears,
    Were left to heaven's bright rain;
Fresh hopes were born for other years—
    He never smiled again.

                F. D. HEMANS.

VISION OF BELSHAZZAR.

THE King was on his throne,
    The Satraps throng'd the hall;
A thousand bright lamps shone
    O'er that high festival.
A thousand cups of gold,
    In Judah deem'd divine—
Jehovah's vessels hold
    The godless Heathen's wine.

In that same hour and hall,
    The fingers of a hand
Came forth against the wall,
    And wrote as if on sand:
The fingers of a man;—
    A solitary hand
Along the letters ran,
    And traced them like a wand.

The monarch saw, and shook,
  And bade no more rejoice;
All bloodless wax'd his look,
  And tremulous his voice.
" Let the men of lore appear,
  The wisest of the earth,
And expound the words of fear,
  Which mar our royal mirth."

Chaldea's seers are good,
  But here they have no skill;
And the unknown letters stood
  Untold and awful still.
And Babel's men of age
  Are wise and deep in lore;
But now they were not sage,
  They saw—but knew no more.

A captive in the land,
  A stranger and a youth,
He heard the king's command,
  He saw that writing's truth,
The lamps around were bright,
  The prophecy in view;
He read it on that night,—
  The morrow proved it true.

" Belshazzar's grave is made,
  His kingdom pass'd away,
He, in the balance weigh'd,
  Is light and worthless clay,
The shroud, his robe of state,
  His canopy the stone:
The Mede is at his gate!
  The Persian on his throne!"

LORD BYRON.

CASABIANCA.

THE boy stood on the burning deck
    Whence all but he had fled;
The flame that lit the battle's wreck
    Shone round him o'er the dead.

Yet beautiful and bright he stood,
    As born to rule the storm—
A creature of heroic blood,
    A proud though child-like form.

The flames rolled on. He would not go
    Without his father's word;
That father, faint in death below,
    His voice no longer heard.

He called aloud :—" Say, father ! say
    If yet my task is done ! "
He knew not that the chieftain lay
    Unconscious of his son.

" Speak, father ! " once again he cried,
    " If I may yet be gone ! "
And but the booming shots replied,
    And fast the flames rolled on.

Upon his brow he felt their breath,
    And in his waving hair,
And looked from that lone post of death
    In still yet brave despair;

And shouted but once more aloud,
    " My father ! must I stay ? "
While o'er him fast, through sail and shroud
    The wreathing fires made way.

They wrapt the ship in splendour wild,
    They caught the flag on high,
And streamed above the gallant child
    Like banners in the sky.

There came a burst of thunder-sound—
    The boy—oh! where was he?
Ask of the winds that far around
    With fragments strewed the sea!—

With mast, and helm, and pennon fair,
    That well had borne their part;
But the noblest thing which perished there
    Was that young faithful heart!

F. D. HEMANS.

BANNOCKBURN.

Robert Bruce's Address to his Army.

SCOTS, wha hae wi' Wallace bled,
Scots, wham Bruce has aften led;
Welcome to your gory bed,
    Or to glorious victory!

Now's the day, and now's the hour;
See the front o' battle lour;
See approach proud Edward's power—
    Edward! chains and slavery!

Wha will be a traitor knave?
Wha can fill a coward's grave?
Wha sae base as be a slave?
    Traitor! coward! turn, and flee!

Wha for Scotland's king and law
Freedom's sword will strongly draw,
Freeman stand, or freeman fa'?
    Caledonian! on wi' me!

By oppression's woes and pains!
By your sons in servile chains!
We will drain our dearest veins,
    But they shall—they *shall* be free!

Lay the proud usurpers low!
Tyrants fall in every foe!
Liberty 's in every blow!
    Forward! let us do, or die!

                R. BURNS.

NOW.

Rise! for the day is passing,
    And you lie dreaming on;
The others have buckled their armour,
    And forth to the fight are gone:
A place in the ranks awaits you,
    Each man has some part to play;
The Past and the Future are nothing,
    In the face of the stern To-day.

Rise from your dreams of the Future—
    Of gaining some hard-fought field;
Of storming some airy fortress,
    Or bidding some giant yield;
Your Future has deeds of glory,
    Of honour (God grant it may!)
But your arm will never be stronger,
    Or the need so great as To-day.

Rise! if the Past detains you,
    Her sunshine and storms forget;
No chains so unworthy to hold you
    As those of a vain regret:
Sad or bright, she is lifeless ever,
    Cast her phantom arms away,
Nor look back, save to learn the lesson
    Of a nobler strife To-day.

Rise! for the day is passing:
  The sound that you scarcely hear
Is the enemy marching to battle—
  Arise! for the foe is here!
Stay not to sharpen your weapons,
  Or the hour will strike at last,
When, from dreams of a coming battle,
  You may wake to find it past!

A. A. PROCTER.

FLOWERS WITHOUT FRUIT.

PRUNE thou thy words, the thoughts control
  That o'er thee swell and throng;
They will condense within thy soul,
  And change to purpose strong.

But he who lets his feelings run
  In soft luxurious flow,
Shrinks when hard service must be done,
  And faints at every woe.

Faith's meanest deed more favour bears,
  Where hearts and wills are weigh'd,
Than brightest transports, choicest prayers,
  Which bloom their hour and fade.

J. H. NEWMAN.

THE SOLDIER'S DREAM.

OUR bugles sang truce—for the night-cloud had lower'd,
  And the sentinel stars set their watch in the sky;
And thousands had sunk on the ground overpower'd,
  The weary to sleep, and the wounded to die.

When reposing that night on my pallet of straw,
　By the wolf-scaring faggot that guarded the slain
At the dead of the night a sweet vision I saw,
　And thrice ere the morning I dreamt it again.

Methought from the battle-field's dreadful array,
　Far, far I had roam'd on a desolate track:
'Twas Autumn,—and sunshine arose on the way
　To the home of my fathers, that welcomed me back.

I flew to the pleasant fields traversed so oft
　In life's morning march, when my bosom was young;
I heard my own mountain-goats bleating aloft,
　And knew the sweet strain that the corn-reapers sung

Then pledged we the wine-cup, and fondly I swore,
　From my home and my weeping friends never to part;
My little ones kiss'd me a thousand times o'er,
　And my wife sobb'd aloud in her fulness of heart.

Stay, stay with us,—rest, thou art weary and worn;
　And fain was their war-broken soldier to stay;—
But sorrow return'd with the dawning of morn,
　And the voice in my dreaming ear melted away.

　　　　　　　　　　　　　T. CAMPBELL.

———＋———

THE BURIAL OF SIR JOHN MOORE.

NOT a drum was heard, not a funeral note,
　As his corse to the ramparts we hurried;
Not a soldier discharged his farewell shot
　O'er the grave where our hero we buried.

We buried him darkly at dead of night,
　The sods with our bayonets turning;
By the struggling moonbeam's misty light,
　And the lantern dimly burning.

useless coffin enclosed. his breast,
  Not in sheet or in shroud we wound him;
But he lay like a warrior taking his rest,
  With his martial cloak around him.

Few and short were the prayers we said,
  And we spoke not a word of sorrow;
But we stedfastly gazed on the face that was dead,
  And we bitterly thought of the morrow.

We thought, as we hollow'd his narrow bed,
  And smooth'd down his lonely pillow,
That the foe and the stranger would tread o'er his head,
  And we far away on the billow !

Lightly they'll talk of the spirit that's gone,
  And o'er his cold ashes upbraid him,—
But little he'll reck, if they let him sleep on,
  In the grave where a Briton has laid him.

But half of our heavy task was done,
  When the clock struck the hour for retiring;
And we heard the distant and random gun
  That the foe was sullenly firing.

Slowly and sadly we laid him down,
  From the field of his fame fresh and gory;
We carved not a line, and we raised not a stone—
  But we left him alone with his glory !

                                    C. WOLFE.

MAXIMUS.

MANY, if God should make them kings,
  Might not disgrace the throne He gave;
How few who could as well fulfil
  The holier office of a slave.

I hold him great who, for Love's sake,
  Can give, with generous, earnest will,—
Yet he who takes for Love's sweet sake,
  I think I hold more generous still.

I prize the instinct that can turn
  From vain pretence with proud disdain ;
Yet more I prize a simple heart
  Paying credulity with pain.

I bow before the noble mind
  That freely some great wrong forgives ;
Yet nobler is the one forgiven,
  Who bears that burden well, and lives.

It may be hard to gain, and still
  To keep a lowly steadfast heart;
Yet he who loses has to fill
  A harder and a truer part.

Glorious it is to wear the crown
  Of a deserved and pure success ;—
He who knows how to fail has won
  A Crown whose lustre is not less.

Great may he be who can command
  And rule with just and tender sway ;
Yet is diviner wisdom taught
  Better by him who can obey.

Blessèd are those who die for God,
  And earn the Martyr's crown of light—
Yet he who lives for God may be
  A greater Conqueror in His sight.

A. A. PROCTER.

JUDGE NOT.

JUDGE not; the workings of his brain
  And of his heart thou canst not see;
What looks to thy dim eyes a stain,
  In God's pure light may only be
A scar, brought from some well-won field,
Where thou wouldst only faint and yield.

The look, the air, that frets thy sight,
  May be a token, that below
The soul has closed in deadly fight
  With some infernal fiery foe,
Whose glance would scorch thy smiling grace,
And cast thee shuddering on thy face!

The fall thou darest to despise—
  May be the slackened angel's hand
Has suffered it, that he may rise
  And take a firmer, surer stand;
Or, trusting less to earthly things,
May henceforth learn to use his wings.

And judge none lost; but wait, and see,
  With hopeful pity, not disdain;
The depth of the abyss may be
  The measure of the height of pain
And love and glory that may raise
This soul to God in after days!

A. A. PROCTER.

THE LIGHT OF STARS.

THE night is come, but not too soon;
  And sinking silently,
All silently, the little moon
  Drops down behind the sky.

There is no light in earth or heaven,
  But the cold light of stars ;
And the first watch of night is given
  To the red planet Mars.

Is it the tender star of love ?
  The star of love and dreams ?
Oh no ! from that blue tent above,
  A hero's armour gleams.

And earnest thoughts within me rise,
  When I behold afar,
Suspended in the evening skies,
  The shield of that red star.

O star of strength ! I see thee stand
  And smile upon my pain ;
Thou beckonest with thy mailèd hand,
  And I am strong again.

Within my breast there is no light,
  But the cold light of stars ;
I give the first watch of the night
  To the red planet Mars.

The star of the unconquered will,
  He rises in my breast,
Serene, and resolute, and still,
  And calm, and self-possessed.

And thou, too, whosoe'er thou art,
  That readest this brief psalm,
As one by one thy hopes depart,
  Be resolute and calm.

Oh fear not in a world like this,
  And thou shalt know ere long,
Know how sublime a thing it is
  To suffer and be strong.
                    H. W. Longfellow.

THE FLIGHT OF XERXES.

I saw him on the battle-eve,
  When, like a king, he bore him,—
Proud hosts in glittering helm and greave,
  And prouder chiefs before him:
The warrior, and the warrior's deeds—
The morrow, and the morrow's meeds,—
  No daunting thoughts came o'er him ;—
He looked around him, and his eye
Defiance flashed to earth and sky.

He looked on ocean :—its broad breast
  Was covered with his fleet ;
On earth :—and saw from east to west
  His bannered millions meet ;
While rock, and glen, and cave, and coast,
Shook with the war-cry of that host,
  The thunder of their feet !
He heard the imperial echoes ring ;
He heard, and *felt* himself a king.

I saw him next alone :—nor camp
  Nor chief, his steps attended,
Nor banners blazed, nor courser's tramp
  With war-cries proudly blended.
He stood alone, whom Fortune high
So lately seemed to deify ;
  He, who with Heaven contended,
Fled like a fugitive and slave !
Behind, the foe ;—before, the wave.

He stood ;—fleet, army, treasure gone,
  Alone, and in despair !
But wave and wind swept ruthless on,
  For *they* were monarchs there ;

And Xerxes, in a single bark,
Where late his thousand ships were dark,
   Must all their fury dare ;—
Thy glorious revenge was this !
Thy trophy, deathless Salamis !

                  M. J. JEWSBURY.

ELIZABETH AT TILBURY.

Autumn, 1588.

LET them come, come never so proudly,
  O'er the green waves in tall array ;
Silver clarions menacing loudly,
  " All the Spains " on their pennons gay ;
High on deck of their gilded galleys
  Our light sailers they scorn below :—
We will scatter them, plague, and shatter them,
  Till their flag hauls down to the foe !
      For our oath we swear
      By the name we bear,
By England's Queen and England free and fair,—
Hers ever and hers still, come life, come death :
    God save Elizabeth !

Sidonia, Recalde, and Leyva
  Watch from their bulwarks in swarthy scorn ;
Lords and Princes by Philip's favour :
  We by birthright are noble born !
Freemen born of the blood of freemen,
  Sons of Cressy and Flodden are we :
We shall sunder them, fire, and plunder them,—
  English boats on the English sea !
      And our oath we swear
      By the name we bear,
By England's Queen and England free and fair,—
Hers ever and hers still, come life, come death :
    God save Elizabeth !

                      D

Drake and Frobisher, Hawkins and Howard,
　Raleigh, Cavendish, Cecil and Brooke,
Hang like wasps by the flagships tower'd,
　Sting their way through the thrice-piled oak :—
Let them range their seven-mile crescent,
　Giant galleons, canvas wide !
Ours will harry them, board, and carry them,
　Plucking the plumes of the Spanish pride.
　　　　For our oath we swear
　　　　By the name we bear,
By England's Queen and England free and fair,—
Hers ever and hers still, come life, come death :
　　　　God save Elizabeth !

—Has God risen in wrath and scatter'd,
　Have His tempests smote them in scorn ?
Past the Orcades, dumb and tatter'd,
　'Mong sea-beasts do they drift forlorn ?
We were as lions hungry for battle ;
　God has made our battle His own !
God has scatter'd them, sunk, and shatter'd them :
　Give the glory to Him alone !
　　　　With our oath we swear
　　　　By the name we bear,
By England's Queen and England free and fair,—
Hers ever and hers still, come life, come death :
　　　　God save Elizabeth !

　　　　　　　　　F. T. PALGRAVE.

LOCHINVAR.

O, young Lochinvar is come out of the west,
Through all the wide Border his steed was the best,
And save his good broadsword, he weapons had none,
He rode all unarm'd, and he rode all alone.
So faithful in love, and so dauntless in war,
There never was knight like the young Lochinvar.

He staid not for brake, and he stopp'd not for stone,
He swam the Eske river where ford there was none;
But ere he alighted at Netherby gate,
The bride had consented, the gallant came late;
For a laggard in love, and a dastard in war,
Was to wed the fair Ellen of brave Lochinvar.

So boldly he enter'd the Netherby Hall,
Among bride's-men, and kinsmen, and brothers, and all:
Then spoke the bride's father, his hand on his sword,
(For the poor craven bridegroom said never a word,)
"O come ye in peace here, or come ye in war,
Or to dance at our bridal, young Lord Lochinvar?"—

"I long woo'd your daughter, my suit you denied;—
Love swells like the Solway, but ebbs like its tide—
And now am I come, with this lost love of mine,
To lead but one measure, drink one cup of wine.
There are maidens in Scotland more lovely by far,
That would gladly be bride to the young Lochinvar."

The bride kiss'd the goblet: the knight took it up,
He quaff'd off the wine, and he threw down the cup.
She look'd down to blush, and she look'd up to sigh,
With a smile on her lips, and a tear in her eye.
He took her soft hand, ere her mother could bar,—
"Now tread we a measure!" said young Lochinvar.

So stately his form, and so lovely her face,
That never a hall such a galliard did grace;
While her mother did fret, and her father did fume,
And the bridegroom stood dangling his bonnet and plume;
And the bride-maidens whisper'd, "'Twere better by far,
To have match'd our fair cousin with young Lochinvar."

One touch to her hand, and one word in her ear,
When they reach'd the hall-door, and the charger stood
    near;
So light to the croupe the fair lady he swung,
So light to the saddle before her he sprung!

"She is won! we are gone, over bank, bush, and scaur;
They'll have fleet steeds that follow," quoth young
    Lochinvar.

There was mounting 'mong Græmes of the Netherby clan;
Fosters, Fenwicks, and Musgraves, they rode and they ran;
There was racing and chasing, on Cannobie Lee,
But the lost bride of Netherby ne'er did they see.
So daring in love, and so dauntless in war,
Have ye e'er heard of gallant like young Lochinvar?

                            SIR W. SCOTT.

CRESCENTIUS.

I LOOK'D upon his brow,—no sign
  Of guilt or fear was there;
He stood as proud by that death-shrine
  As even o'er Despair
He had a power; in his eye
There was a quenchless energy,
  A spirit that could dare
The deadliest form that death could take,
And dare it for the daring's sake.

He stood, the fetters on his hand,—
  He raised them haughtily;
And had that grasp been on the brand,
  It could not wave on high
With freer pride than it waved now.
Around he look'd with changeless brow
  On many a torture nigh:
The rack, the chain, the axe, the wheel,
And, worst of all, his own red steel.

I saw him once before; he rode
  Upon a coal-black steed,
And tens of thousands throng'd the road
' And bade their warrior speed.

His helm, his breast-plate were of gold,
And graved with many a dent that told
   Of many a soldier's deed ;
The sun shone on his sparkling mail,
And danced his snow-plume on the gale.

But now he stood chain'd and alone,
   The headsman by his side,
The plume, the helm, the charger, gone ;
   The sword which had defied
The mightiest, lay broken near ;
And yet no sign or sound of fear
   Came from that lip of pride ;
And never king or conqueror's brow
Wore higher look than his did now.

He bent beneath the headsman's stroke
   With an uncover'd eye ;
A wild shout from the numbers broke
   Who throng'd to see him die.
It was a people's loud acclaim,
The voice of anger and of shame,
   A nation's funeral cry,
Rome's wail above her only son,
Her patriot, and her latest one.

                      L. E. LANDON.

THE CURFEW SONG OF ENGLAND.

HARK ! from the dim church-tower,
   The deep slow Curfew's chime !—
A heavy sound unto hall and bower
   In England's olden time !
Sadly 'twas heard by him who came
   From the fields of his toil at night,
And who might not see his own hearth-flame
   In his children's eyes make light.

Sternly and sadly heard,
  As it quenched the wood-fire's glow,
Which had cheered the board with the mirthful word,
  And the red wine's foaming flow;
Until that sullen boding knell,
  Flung out from every fane,
On harp, and lip, and spirit fell,
  With a weight and with a chain.

Woe for the pilgrim then
  In the wild-deer's forest far!
No cottage lamp to the haunts of men
  Might guide him, as a star.
And woe for him whose wakeful soul,
  With lone aspirings filled,
Would have lived o'er some immortal scroll,
  While the sounds of earth were stilled!

And yet a deeper woe
  For the watcher by the bed,
Where the fondly-loved in pain lay low,
  In pain and sleepless dread!
For the mother, doomed unseen to keep
  By the dying babe her place,
And to feel its sleeping pulse, and weep,
  Yet not behold its face!

Darkness in chieftain's hall!
  Darkness in peasant's cot!
While Freedom, under that shadowy pall,
  Sat mourning o'er her lot.
Oh! the fireside's peace we well may prize!
  For blood hath flowed like rain,
Poured forth to make sweet sanctuaries
  Of England's homes again.

Heap the yule-faggots high
  Till the red light fills the room!
It is Home's own hour when the stormy sky
  Grows thick with evening gloom.

Gather ye round the holy hearth !
 And by its gladdening blaze,
Unto thankful bliss we will change our mirth,
 With a thought of the olden days.

F. D. HEMANS.

THE SICILIAN VESPERS.

SILENCE o'er sea and earth
 With the veil of evening fell,
Till the convent tower sent deeply forth
 The chime of its vesper bell.
One moment, and that solemn sound
 Fell heavily on the ear ;
But a sterner echo passed around,
 Which the boldest shook to hear.

The startled monks thronged up
 In the torchlight cold and dim ;
And the priest let fall his incense-cup,
 And the virgin hushed her hymn ;
For a boding clash, and a clanging tramp,
 And a summoning voice were heard,
And fretted wall and tombstone damp
 To the fearful echo stirred.

The peasant heard the sound
 As he sat beside his hearth ;
And the song and the dance were hushed around,
 With the fireside tale of mirth.
The chieftain shook in his bannered hall
 As the sound of war drew nigh ;
And the warder shrank from the castle wall
 As the gleam of spears went by.

Woe, woe to the stranger, then,
  At the feast and flow of wine,
In the red array of mailèd men,
  Or bowed at the holy shrine;
For the wakened pride of an injured land
  Had burst its iron thrall;
From the plumèd chief to the pilgrim band,
  Woe, woe to the sons of Gaul!

Proud beings tell that hour
  With the young and passing fair,
And the flame went up from dome and tower,
  The avenger's arm was there!
The stranger priest at the altar stood,
  And clasped his beads in prayer;
But the holy shrine grew dim with blood,—
  The avenger found him there!

Woe, woe to the sons of Gaul,
  To the serf and mailèd lord;
They were gathered darkly, one and all,
  To the harvest of the sword;
And the morning sun, with a quiet smile,
  Shone out o'er hill and glen,
O'er ruined temple, and mouldering pile,
  And the ghastly forms of men.

Ay, the sunshine sweetly smiled,
  As its early glance came forth;
It had no sympathy with the wild
  And terrible things of earth;
And the man of blood that day might read
  In a language, freely given,
How ill his dark and midnight deed
  Became the light of heaven.

                          J. G. WHITTIER.

ADIEU.

LET time and chance combine, combine,
Let time and chance combine ;
The fairest love from heaven above,
That love of yours was mine,
         My dear,
That love of yours was mine.

The past is fled and gone, and gone,
The past is fled and gone ;
If naught but pain to me remain,
I'll fare in memory on,
         My dear,
I'll fare in memory on.

The saddest tears must fall, must fall,
The saddest tears must fall ;
In weal or woe, in this world below,
I love you ever and all,
         My dear,
I love you ever and all.

A long road full of pain, of pain,
A long road full of pain ;
One soul, one heart, sworn ne'er to part,—
We ne'er can meet again,
         My dear,
We ne'er can meet again.

Hard fate will not allow, allow,
Hard fate will not allow ;
We blessed were as the angels are,—
Adieu forever now,
         My dear,
Adieu forever now.

               T. CARLYLE.

A HIGHLAND BOAT SONG.

HAIL to the Chief who in triumph advances!
  Honour'd and bless'd be the ever-green Pine!
Long may the tree, in his banner that glances,
  Flourish, the shelter and grace of our line!
      Heaven send it happy dew,
      Earth lend it sap anew,
Gaily to bourgeon, and broadly to grow,
      While every Highland glen
      Sends our shout back agen,
" Roderigh Vich Alpine dhu, ho! ieroe! "

Ours is no sapling, chance-sown by the fountain,
  Blooming at Beltane, in winter to fade;
When the whirlwind has stripp'd every leaf on th
      mountain,
  The more shall Clan-Alpine exult in her shade.
      Moor'd in the rifted rock,
      Proof to the tempest's shock,
Firmer he roots him the ruder it blow;
      Menteith and Breadalbane, then,
      Echo his praise agen,
" Roderigh Vich Alpine dhu, ho! ieroe! "

Proudly our pibroch has thrill'd in Glen Fruin,
  And Bannochar's groans to our slogan replied;
Glen Luss and Ross-dhu, they are smoking in ruin,
  And the best of Loch-Lomond lie dead on her side.
      Widow and Saxon maid
      Long shall lament our raid,
Think of Clan-Alpine with fear and with woe;
      Lennox and Leven-glen
      Shake when they hear agen,
" Roderigh Vich Alpine dhu, ho! ieroe! "

Row, vassals, row, for the pride of the Highlands!
   Stretch to your oars, for the ever-green Pine!
O, that the rose-bud that graces yon islands,
   Were wreathed in a garland around him to twine!
      O that some seedling gem,
      Worthy such noble stem,
Honour'd and bless'd in their shadow might grow!
     Loud should Clan-Alpine then
     Ring from her deepmost glen,
" Roderigh Vich Alpine dhu, ho! ieroe!"

SIR W. SCOTT.

DOWN ON THE SHORE.

Down on the shore, on the sunny shore!
   Where the salt smell cheers the land;
Where the tide moves bright under boundless light,
   And the surge on the glittering strand;
Where the children wade in the shallow pools,
   Or run from the froth in play;
Where the swift little boats with milk-white wings
   Are crossing the sapphire bay,
And the ship in full sail, with a fortunate gale,
   Holds proudly on her way.
Where the nets are spread on the grass to dry,
And asleep, hard by, the fishermen lie,
Under the tent of the warm blue sky,
With the hushing wave on its golden floor
      To sing their lullaby.

Down on the shore, on the stormy shore!
   Beset by a growling sea,
Whose mad waves leap on the rocky steep
   Like wolves up a traveller's tree.
Where the foam flies wide, and an angry blast
   Blows the curlew off, with a screech;
Where the brown sea-wrack, torn up by the roots,
   Is flung out of fishes' reach;

Where the tall ship rolls on the hidden shoals,
  And scatters her planks on the beach, .
Where slate and straw through the village spin,
And a cottage fronts the fiercest din
With a sailor's wife sitting sad within,
Hearkening the wind and water's roar,
      Till at last her tears begin.

W. ALLINGHAM.

"SPEAK KINDLY."

DEAL gently with the erring!
  Ye may not know the power
With which the dark temptation came
  In some unguarded hour.
Ye may not know how earnestly
  He struggled, or how well,
Until the hour of darkness came,
  And sadly thus he fell.

Think kindly of the erring!
  Oh, do not thou forget!
However darkly stain'd by sin,
  He is thy brother yet!
Heir of the self-same heritage,
  Child of the self-same God;
He hath but stumbled in the path
  Thou hast in weakness trod.

Speak gently to the erring!
  For is it not enough
That innocence and peace have gone,
  Without thy censure rough?
It sure must be a weary lot,
  That sin-crush'd heart to bear,
And they who share a happier fate,
  Their chidings well may spare.

Oh, kindly *help* the erring!
 Thou yet may'st lead him back,
With gracious words and tones of love,
 From mis'ry's thorny track.
Forget not thou hast often sinned,
 And sinful yet must be,—
Deal gently with the erring one,
 As God hath dealt with thee!

WOODMAN.

BE STRONG.

BE strong to *hope*, oh Heart!
 Though day is bright,
The stars can only shine
 In the dark night.
Be strong, oh Heart of mine,
 Look towards the light!

Be strong to *bear*, oh Heart!
 Nothing is vain:
Strive not, for life is care,
 And God sends pain,
Heaven is above, and there
 Rest will remain!

Be strong to *love*, oh Heart!
 Love knows not wrong,
Didst thou love—creatures even,
 Life were not long;
Didst thou love God in Heaven,
 Thou wouldst be strong!

A. A. PROCTER.

SONG FOR AUGUST.

BENEATH this starry arch,
  Nought resteth or is still;
But all things hold their march
  As if by one great will.
    Moves one, move all;
    Hark to the foot-fall!
      On, on, for ever.

Yon sheaves were once but seed;
Will ripens into deed;
As cave-drops swell the streams,
Day thoughts feed nightly dreams;
And sorrow tracketh wrong,
As echo follows song,
      On, on, for ever.

By night, like stars on high,
  The hours reveal their train;
They whisper and go by;
  I never watch in vain.
    Moves one, move all;
    Hark to the foot-fall!
      On, on, for ever.

They pass the cradle head,
  And there a promise shed;
They pass the moist, new grave,
  And bid rank verdure wave;
    They bear through every clime,
    The harvests of all time,
      On, on, for ever.

                  H. MARTINEAU.

THE ROVER.

" A WEARY lot is thine, fair maid,
   A weary lot is thine!
To pull the thorn thy brow to braid,
   And press the rue for wine!
A lightsome eye, a soldier's mien,
   A feather of the blue,
A doublet of the Lincoln green,—
No more of me you knew,
      My love!
No more of me you knew.

" This morn is merry June, I trow,
   The rose is budding fain;
But she shall bloom in winter snow,
   Ere we two meet again."
He turn'd his charger as he spake,
   Upon the river shore,
He gave his bridle-reins a shake,
Said, "Adieu for evermore,
      My love!
And adieu for evermore."

                    SIR W. SCOTT.

ALONG THE SHORE.

ALONG the shore, along the shore
   I see the wavelets meeting:
But thee I see—ah, never more,
   For all my wild heart's beating.
The little wavelets come and go,
The tide of life ebbs to and fro,
   Advancing and retreating:
But from the shore, the changeless shore,
   The sea is parted never:
And mine I hold thee evermore,
   For ever and for ever.

Along the shore, along the shore,
  I hear the waves resounding,
But thou wilt cross them never more,
  For all my wild heart's bounding:
The moon comes out above the tide,
And quiets all the billows wide
  Her pathway bright surrounding:
Thus on the shore, the dreary shore,
  I walk with weak endeavour;
I have thy love's light evermore,
  For ever and for ever.

D. M. CRAIK.

THE BUILDERS.

ALL are architects of Fate,
  Working in these walls of Time;
Some with massive deeds and great,
  Some with ornaments of rhyme.

Nothing useless is, or low;
  Each thing in its place is best;
And what seems but idle show
  Strengthens and supports the rest.

For the structure that we raise,
  Time is with materials filled;
Our to-days and yesterdays
  Are the blocks with which we build.

Truly shape and fashion these;
  Leave no yawning gaps between;
Think not, because no man sees,
  Such things will remain unseen.

In the elder days of Art,
  Builders wrought with greatest care
Each minute and unseen part;
  For the Gods see everywhere.

Let us do our work as well,
  Both the unseen and the seen;
Make the house, where Gods may dwell,
  Beautiful, entire, and clean.

Else our lives are incomplete,
  Standing in these walls of Time,
Broken stairways, where the feet
  Stumble as they seek to climb.

Build to-day, then, strong and sure,
  With a firm and ample base;
And ascending and secure
  Shall to-morrow find its place.

Thus alone can we attain
  To those turrets, where the eye
Sees the world as one vast plain,
  And one boundless reach of sky.

                    H. W. LONGFELLOW.

THE BATTLE OF MORGARTEN.

THE wine-month shone in its golden prime,
  And the red grapes clustering hung,
But a deeper sound through the Switzer's clime,
  Than the vintage-music, rung;
    A sound, through vaulted cave,
    A sound, through echoing glen,
  Like the hollow swell of a rushing wave;
    'Twas the tread of steel-girt men.

And a trumpet, pealing wide and far,
  'Midst the ancient rocks was blown,
Till the Alps replied to that voice of war,
  With a thousand of their own.

                                    E

And through the forest-glooms
  Flashed helmets to the day,
And the winds were tossing knightly plumes,
  Like the larch-boughs in their play.

In Hasli's wilds there was gleaming steel,
  As the host of the Austrian passed ;
And the Schreckhorn's rocks, with a savage peal,
  Made mirth of his clarion's blast.
    Up 'midst the Righi snows,
    The stormy march was heard,
  With the charger's tramp, whence fire-sparks rose,
    And the leader's gathering word.

But a band, the noblest band of all,
  Through the rude Morgarten strait,
With blazoned streamers, and lances tall,
  Moved onwards, in princely state.
    They came with heavy chains,
    For the race despised so long ;
  But amidst his Alp-domains
    The herdsman's arm is strong !

The sun was reddening the clouds of morn
  When they entered the rock-defile,
And shrill as a joyous hunter's horn
  Their bugles rung the while.
    But on the misty height,
    Where the mountain-people stood,
  There was stillness, as of night,
    When storms at a distance brood.

There was stillness, as of deep dead night,
  And a pause,—but not of fear,
While the Switzers gazed on the gathering might
  Of the hostile shield and spear.
    On wound those columns bright
    Between the lake and wood,
  But they looked not to the misty height
    Where the mountain people stood.

The pass was filled with their serried power,
  All helmed and mail-arrayed,
And their steps had sounds like a thunder-shower
  In the rustling forest-shade.
    There were prince and crested knight,
    Hemmed in by cliff and flood,
  When a shout arose from the misty height
    Where the mountain people stood.

And the mighty rocks came bounding down,
  Their startled foes among,
With a joyous whirl from the summit thrown—
  Oh! the herdsman's arm is strong!
    They came like lauwine hurled
    From Alp to Alp in play,
  When the echoes shout through the snowy world,
    And the pines are borne away.

The fir-woods crashed on the mountain side,
  And the Switzers rushed from high,
With a sudden charge, on the flower and pride
  Of the Austrian chivalry:
    Like hunters of the deer,
    They stormed the narrow dell,
  And first in the shock, with Uri's spear,
    Was the arm of William Toll.

There was tumult in the crowded strait,
  And a cry of wild dismay,
And many a warrior met his fate
  From a peasant's hand that day!
    And the empire's banner then
    From its place of waving free
  Went down before the shepherd-men,
    The men of the Forest-sea.

With their pikes and massy clubs they brake
  The cuirass and the shield,
And the war-horse dashed to the reddening lake
  From the reapers of the field!

The field—but not of sheaves—
Proud crests and pennons lay,
Strewn o'er it thick as the birch-wood leaves,
In the autumn tempest's way.

Oh ! the sun in heaven fierce havoc viewed,
When the Austrian turned to fly,
And the brave, in the trampling multitude,
Had a fearful death to die !
And the leader of the war
At eve unhelmed was seen,
With a hurrying step on the wilds afar,
And a pale and troubled mien.

But the sons of the land which the freeman tills,
Went back from the battle-toil,
To their cabin homes 'midst the deep green hills,
All burdened with royal spoil.
There were songs and festal fires
On the soaring Alps that night,
When children sprung to greet their sires
From the wild Morgarten fight.

                              F. D. HEMANS.

————•————

SATURDAY AFTERNOON.

I LOVE to look on a scene like this,
Of wild and careless play,
And persuade myself that I am not old,
And my locks are not yet gray ;
For it stirs the blood in an old man's heart,
And makes his pulses fly,
To catch the thrill of a happy voice,
And the light of a pleasant eye.

I have walk'd the earth for fourscore years ;
And they say that I am old,
That my heart is ripe for the reaper, Death,
And my years are well-nigh told.

It is very true; it is very true;
  I'm old, and "I bide my time:"
But my heart will leap at a scene like this,
  And I half renew my prime.

Play on, play on; I am with you there,
  In the midst of your merry ring;
I can feel the thrill of the daring jump,
  And the rush of the breathless swing.
I hide with you in the fragrant hay,
  And I whoop the smother'd call,
And my feet slip up on the seedy floor,
  And I care not for the fall.

I am willing to die when my time shall come,
  And I shall be glad to go;
For the world at best is a weary place,
  And my pulse is getting low;
But the grave is dark, and the heart will fail
  In treading its gloomy way;
And it wiles my heart from its dreariness,
  To see the young so gay.

N. P. WILLIS.

THE FROST SPIRIT.

HE comes,—he comes,—the Frost Spirit comes!
  You may trace his footsteps now
On the naked woods and the blasted fields
  And the brown hill's withered brow.
He has smitten the leaves of the gray old trees
  Where their pleasant green came forth,
And the winds, which follow wherever he goes,
  Have shaken them down to earth.

He comes,—he comes,—the Frost Spirit comes!—
  From the frozen Labrador,—
From the icy bridge of the Northern seas,
  Which the white bear wanders o'er,—
Where the fisherman's sail is stiff with ice,
  And the luckless forms below
In the sunless cold of the lingering night
  Into marble statues grow!

He comes,—he comes,—the Frost Spirit comes!—
  On the rushing Northern blast,
And the dark Norwegian pines have bowed
  As his fearful breath went past.
With an unscorched wing he has hurried on,
  Where the fires of Hecla glow
On the darkly beautiful sky above
  And the ancient ice below.

He comes,—he comes,—the Frost Spirit comes!—
  And the quiet lake shall feel
The torpid touch of his glazing breath,
  And ring to the skater's heel;
And the streams which danced on the broken rocks,
  Or sang to the leaning grass,
Shall bow again to the winter chain,
  And in mournful silence pass.

He comes,—he comes,—the Frost Spirit comes!—
  Let us meet him as we may,
And turn with the light of the parlour fire
  His evil power away;
And gather closer the circle round,
  When that fire-light dances high,
And laugh at the shriek of the baffled Fiend
  As his sounding wing goes by!

J. G. WHITTIER.

ONE BY ONE.

One by one the sands are flowing,
  One by one the moments fall;
Some are coming, some are going;
  Do not strive to grasp them all.

One by one thy duties wait thee,
  Let thy whole strength go to each,
Let no future dreams elate thee,
  Learn thou first what these can teach.

One by one (bright gifts from Heaven)
  Joys are sent thee here below;
Take them readily when given,
  Ready too to let them go.

One by one thy griefs shall meet thee,
  Do not fear an armèd band;
One will fade as others greet thee;
  Shadows passing through the land.

Do not look at life's long sorrow;
  See how small each moment's pain;
God will help thee for to-morrow,
  So each day begin again.

Every hour that fleets so slowly
  Has its task to do or bear;
Luminous the crown, and holy,
  When each gem is set with care.

Do not linger with regretting,
  Or for passing hours despond;
Nor, the daily toil forgetting,
  Look too eagerly beyond.

Hours are golden links, God's token,
  Reaching Heaven; but one by one
Take them, lest the chain be broken
  Ere the pilgrimage be done.

                    A. A. PROCTER.

THE BATTLE OF HOHENLINDEN.

On Linden, when the sun was low,
All bloodless lay the untrodden snow,
And dark as winter was the flow
Of Iser, rolling rapidly.

But Linden saw another sight,
When the drum beat, at dead of night,
Commanding fires of death to light
The darkness of her scenery.

By torch and trumpet fast array'd
Each horseman drew his battle-blade,
And furious every charger neigh'd,
To join the dreadful revelry.

Then shook the hills with thunder riven,
Then rush'd the steed to battle driven,
And louder than the bolts of heaven,
Far flash'd the red artillery.

But redder yet that light shall glow,
On Linden's hills of stainèd snow,
And bloodier yet the torrent flow
Of Iser, rolling rapidly.

'Tis morn, but scarce yon level sun
Can pierce the war-clouds, rolling dun,
When furious Frank, and fiery Hun,
Shout in their sulph'rous canopy.

The combat deepens.　On, ye brave,
Who rush to glory, or the grave!
Wave, Munich! all thy banners wave!
And charge with all thy chivalry!

Few, few, shall part where many meet!
The snow shall be their winding-sheet!
And every turf beneath their feet
Shall be a soldier's sepulchre.

T. CAMPBELL.

₂YE MARINERS OF ENGLAND.

Ye mariners of England!
That guard our native seas;
Whose flag has braved, a thousand years,
The battle and the breeze!
Your glorious standard launch again
To match another foe!
And sweep through the deep,
While the stormy tempests blow;
While the battle rages loud and long,
And the stormy tempests blow.

The spirits of your fathers
Shall start from every wave!
For the deck it was their field of fame,
And ocean was their grave;
Where Blake and mighty Nelson fell,
Your manly hearts shall glow,
As ye sweep through the deep,
While the stormy tempests blow;
While the battle rages loud and long,
And the stormy tempests blow.

Britannia needs no bulwark,
No towers along the steep;
Her march is o'er the mountain waves,
Her home is on the deep.
With thunders from her native oak,
She quells the floods below,
As they roar on the shore,
When the stormy tempests blow;
When the battle rages loud and long,
And the stormy tempests blow.

The meteor-flag of England
Shall yet terrific burn;
Till danger's troubled night depart,
And the star of peace return.

Then, then, ye ocean warriors !
Our song and feast shall flow
To the fame of your name,
When the storm has ceased to blow ;
When the fiery fight is heard no more,
And the storm has ceased to blow.

T. CAMPBELL.

BERNARDO AND ALPHONSO.

WITH some good ten of his chosen men,
　Bernardo hath appeared
Before them all in the palace hall,
　The lying King to beard ;
With cap in hand and eye on ground,
　He came in reverend guise,
But ever and anon he frowned,
　And flame broke from his eyes.

" A curse upon thee," cries the King,
　" Who comest unbid to me ;
But what from traitor's blood should spring,
　Save traitors like to thee ?
His sire, lords, had a traitor's heart ;
　Perchance our champion brave
May think it were a pious part
　To share Don Sancho's grave."

" Whoever told this tale the King
　Hath rashness to repeat,"
Cries Bernard, " here my gage I fling
　Before *the liar's* feet.
No treason was in Sancho's blood,
　No stain in mine doth lie :
Below the throne what knight will own
　The coward calumny ?

" The blood that I like water shed,
　When Roland did advance,
By secret traitors hired and led,
　To make us slaves of France ;

The life of King Alphonso
  I saved at Roncesval,—
Your words, Lord King, are recompense
  Abundant for it all.

" Your horse was down,— your hope was flown,—
  I saw the falchion shine,
That soon had drunk your royal blood,
  Had I not ventured mine ;
But memory soon of service done
  Deserteth the ingrate ;
You've thanked the son for life and crown
  By the father's bloody fate.

" Ye swore upon your kingly faith,
  To set Don Sancho free ;
But, curse upon your paltering breath,
  The light he ne'er did see ;
He died in dungeon cold and dim,
  By Alphonso's base decree,
And visage blind, and mangled limb,
  Were all they gave to me.

" The king that swerveth from his word,
  Hath stained his purple black :
No Spanish lord will draw the sword
  Behind a liar's back ;
But noble vengeance shall be mine,
  An open hate I'll shew,—
The King hath injured Carpio's line,
  And Bernard is his foe."

" Seize, seize him ! " loud the King doth scream :
  " There are a thousand here !
Let his foul blood this instant stream :—
  What ! caitiffs, do ye fear?
Seize, seize the traitor ! "—But not one
  To move a finger dareth ;
Bernardo standeth by the throne,
  And calm his sword he bareth.

He drew the falchion from the sheath,
    And held it up on high,
And all the hall was still as death :—
    Cries Bernard, " Here am I,—
And here is the sword that owns no lord,
    Excepting heaven and me ;
Fain would I know who dares its point,—
    King, Condé, or Grandee."

Then to his mouth the horn he drew
    (It hung below his cloak);
His ten true men the signal knew,
    And through the ring they broke;
With helm on head, and blade in hand,
    The knights the circle brake,
And back the lordlings 'gan to stand,
    And the false King to quake.

" Ha ! Bernard," quoth Alphonso,
    " What means this warlike guise ?
Ye know full well I jested,—
    Ye know your worth I prize."
But Bernard turned upon his heel,
    And smiling passed away :—
Long rued Alphonso and his realm
    The jesting of that day.

                            J. G. LOCKHART.

VICTOR GALBRAITH.

UNDER the walls of Monterey
At daybreak the bugles began to play,
    Victor Galbraith !
In the mist of the morning damp and gray,
These were the words they seemed to say :
    ."Come forth to thy death,
    Victor Galbraith ! "

Forth he came, with a martial tread;
Firm was his step, erect his head;
    Victor Galbraith!
He who so well the bugle played,
Could not mistake the words it said:
    "Come forth to thy death,
    Victor Galbraith!"

He looked at the earth, he looked at the sky,
He looked at the files of musketry,
    Victor Galbraith!
And he said, with a steady voice and eye,
"Take good aim; I am ready to die!"
    Thus challenges death
    Victor Galbraith.

Twelve fiery tongues flashed straight and red,
Six leaden balls on their errand sped;
    Victor Galbraith
Falls to the ground, but he is not dead:
His name was not stamped on those balls of lead,
    And they only scathe
    Victor Galbraith.

Three balls are in his breast and brain,
But he rises out of the dust again,
    Victor Galbraith!
The water he drinks has a bloody stain;
"O kill me, and put me out of my pain!"
    In his agony prayeth
    Victor Galbraith.

Forth dart once more those tongues of flame,
And the bugler has died a death of shame,
    Victor Galbraith!
His soul has gone back to whence it came,
And no one answers to the name,
    When the Sergeant saith,
    "Victor Galbraith!"

Under the walls of Monterey
By night a bugle is heard to play,
   Victor Galbraith!
Through the mist of the valley damp and gray
The sentinels hear the sound, and say,
   "That is the wraith
   Of Victor Galbraith!"

               H. W. LONGFELLOW.

THE BURIAL OF THE CHAMPION OF HIS CLASS, AT YALE COLLEGE.

YE'VE gather'd to your place of prayer
   With slow and measured tread;
Your ranks are full, your mates are there—
   But the soul of one has fled.
He was the proudest in his strength,
   The manliest of ye all;
Why lies he at that fearful length,
   And ye around his pall?

Ye reckon it in days, since he
   Strode up that foot-worn aisle,
With his dark eye flashing gloriously,
   And his lip wreathed with a smile.
O, had it been but told you, then,
   To mark whose lamp was dim—
From out yon rank of fresh-lipp'd men,
   Would ye have singled him?

Whose was the sinewy arm, that flung
   Defiance to the ring?
Whose laugh of victory loudest rung—
   Yet not for glorying?
Whose heart, in generous deed and thought,
   No rivalry might brook,
And yet distinction claiming not?
   There lies he—go and look!

On now—his requiem is done,
　The last deep prayer is said—
On to his burial, comrades—on,
　With a friend and brother dead!
Slow—for it presses heavily—
　It is a man ye bear!
Slow, for our thoughts dwell wearily
　On the gallant sleeper there.

Tread lightly, comrades!—we have laid
　His dark locks on his brow—
Like life—save deeper light and shade:
　We'll not disturb them now.
Tread lightly—for 'tis beautiful,
　That blue-vein'd eyelid's sleep,
Hiding the eye death left so dull—
　Its slumber we will keep.

Rest now! his journeying is done—
　Your feet are on his sod—
Death's blow has fell'd your champion—
　He waiteth here his God.
Ay—turn and weep—'tis manliness
　To be heart-broken here—
For the grave of one, the best of us,
　Is water'd by the tear.

N. P. WILLIS.

BOADICEA.

WHEN the British warrior queen,
　Bleeding from the Roman rods,
Sought, with an indignant mien,
　Counsel of her country's gods,

Sage beneath the spreading oak
　Sat the Druid, hoary chief;
Ev'ry burning word he spoke
　Full of rage, and full of grief.

" Princess ! if our aged eyes
  Weep upon thy matchless wrongs,
'Tis because resentment ties
  All the terrors of our tongues.

" Rome shall perish—write that word
  In the blood that she has spilt;
Perish, hopeless and abhorr'd,
  Deep in ruin as in guilt.

" Rome, for empire far renown'd,
  Tramples on a thousand states ;
Soon her pride shall kiss the ground—
  Hark ! the Gaul is at her gates !

" Other Romans shall arise,
  Heedless of a soldier's name ;
Sounds, not arms, shall win the prize—
  Harmony the path to fame.

" Then the progeny that springs
  From the forests of our land,
Arm'd with thunder, clad with wings,
  Shall a wider world command.

" Regions Cæsa   ew
  Thy posterity
Where his eagles ʟ
  None invincible as

Such the bard's prophe
  Pregnant with celesti
Bending, as he swept the
  Of his sweet but awfr

She, with all a monarch'ı
  Felt them in her bosoı   ,
Rush'd to battle, fought,   ıed ;
  Dying, hurl'd them at t ɔe.

"Ruffians, pitiless as proud,
  Heav'n awards the vengeance due;
    Empire is on us bestow'd,
    Shame and ruin wait for you."

W. COWPER.

THE SEA FIGHT.

THE Sun hath ridden into the sky,
  And the Night gone to her lair;
    Yet all is asleep
    On the mighty Deep,
And all in the calm gray air.

All seemeth as calm as an infant's dream,
As far as the eye may ken;
    But the cannon blast,
    That just now passed,
Hath awakened ten thousand men.

An order is blown from ship to ship;
All round and round it rings;
    And each sailor is stirred
    By the warlike word,
And his jacket he downwards flings.

He strippeth his arms to his shoulders strong;
He girdeth his loins about;
    And he answers the cry
    Of his foeman nigh,
With a cheer and a noble shout.

What follows?—a puff, and a flash of light,
And the booming of a gun;
    And a scream, that shoots
    To the heart's red roots,
And we know that a fight's begun.

F

A thousand shot are at once let loose;
Each flies from its brazen den
    (Like the Plague's swift breath),
    On its deed of death,
And smites down a file of men.

The guns in their thick-tongued thunder speak,
And the frigates all rock and ride,
    And timbers crash,
    And the mad waves dash
Foaming all far and wide.

And high as the skies run piercing cries,
All telling one tale of woe,—
    That the struggle still,
    Between good and ill,
Goes on, in the earth below.

Day pauses, in gloom, on his western road;
The Moon returns again :
    But, of all who looked bright,
    In the morning light,
There are only a thousand men.

Look up, at the brooding clouds on high ;
Look up, at the awful sun !
    And, behold,—the sea flood
    Is all red with blood :
Hush !—a battle is lost,—and won !
                B. W. Procter.

GELERT'S GRAVE.

The spearman heard the bugle sound,
    And cheerly smiled the morn ;
And many a brach, and many a hound,
    Attend Llewellyn's horn.

And still he blew a louder blast,
　And gave a louder cheer;
"Come, Gelert, why art thou the last
　Llewellyn's horn to hear?

"Oh, where does faithful Gelert roam—
　The flower of all his race;
So true, so brave: a lamb at home,
　A lion in the chase."

'Twas only at Llewellyn's board,
　The faithful Gelert fed;
He watch'd, he serv'd, he cheer'd his lord,
　And sentinell'd his bed.

In sooth, he was a peerless hound,
　The gift of royal John:
But now no Gelert could be found,
　And all the chase rode on.

And now, as over rocks and dells
　The gallant chidings rise,
All Snowdon's craggy chaos y
　With many mingled cries.

That day Llewellyn little loved
　The chase of hart or hare,
And scant and small the booty proved,
　For Gelert was not there.

Unpleased, Llewellyn homeward hied,
　When, near the portal seat,
His truant Gelert he espied,
　Bounding his lord to greet.

But when he gain'd the castle door,
　Aghast the chieftain stood;
The hound was smear'd with gouts of gore,
　His lips and fangs ran blood!

Llewellyn gazed with wild surprise,
    Unused such looks to meet;
His favourite check'd his joyful guise,
    And crouch'd and lick'd his feet.

Onward in haste Llewellyn past,
    And on went Gelert too:
And still where'er his eyes he cast,
    Fresh blood-gouts show'd his view.

O'erturn'd his infant's bed he found,
    The blood-stain'd covert rent;
And all around the walls and ground,
    With recent blood besprent.

He call'd his child; no voice replied;
    He search'd with terror wild;
Blood, Blood, he found on every side,
    But no where found the child!

"Hell-hound, by thee my child's devour'd!"
    The frantic father cried;
And to the hilt the vengeful sword,
    He plunged in Gelert's side.

His suppliant, as to earth he fell,
    No pity could impart;
But still his Gelert's dying yell
    Past heavy o'er his heart.

Aroused by Gelert's dying yell,
    Some slumberer waken'd nigh;
What words the parent's joy can tell,
    To hear his infant cry!

Conceal'd between a mingled heap,
    His hurried search had miss'd;
All glowing from his rosy sleep,
    His cherub boy he kiss'd!

Nor scratch had he, nor harm, nor dread,
. But the same couch beneath
Lay a great wolf, all torn, and dead,
   Tremendous still in death!

Ah! what was then Llewellyn's pain,
   For now the truth was clear;
The gallant hound the wolf had slain,
   To save Llewellyn's heir.

Vain, vain, was all Llewellyn's woe;
   "Best of thy kind, adieu!
The frantic deed which laid thee low,
   This heart shall ever rue!"

And now a gallant tomb they raise,
   With costly sculpture deck'd;
And marbles storied with his praise
   Poor Gelert's bones protect.

Here never could the spearman pass,
   Or forester, unmoved;
Here oft the tear-besprinkled grass,
   Llewellyn's sorrow proved.

And here he hung his horn and spear,
   And oft as evening fell,
In fancy's piercing sounds would hear
   Poor Gelert's dying yell!

And till great Snowdon's rocks grow old,
   And cease the storm to brave,
The consecrated spot shall hold
   The name of Gelert's grave.
                              W. R. SPENCER.

EXCELSIOR.

THE shades of night were falling fast,
As through an Alpine village passed
A youth, who bore, 'mid snow and ice,
A banner with the strange device,
  Excelsior !

His brow was sad ; his eye beneath
Flashed like a falchion from its sheath,
And like a silver clarion rung
The accents of that unknown tongue,
  Excelsior !

In happy homes he saw the light
Of household fires gleam warm and bright
Above, the spectral glaciers shone,
And from his lips escaped a groan,
  Excelsior !

" Try not the Pass ! " the old man said :
" Dark lowers the tempest overhead,
The roaring torrent is deep and wide ! "
And loud that clarion voice replied,
  Excelsior !

" O stay," the maiden said, " and rest
Thy weary head upon this breast ! "
A tear stood in his bright blue eye,
But still he answered, with a sigh,
  Excelsior !

" Beware the pine-tree's withered branch !
Beware the awful avalanche ! "
This was the peasant's last Good-night.
A voice replied, far up the height,
  Excelsior !

At break of day, as heavenward
The pious monks of Saint Bernard
Uttered the oft-repeated prayer,
A voice cried through the startled air,
    Excelsior!

A traveller, by the faithful hound,
Half-buried in the snow was found,
Still grasping in his hand of ice
That banner with the strange device,
    Excelsior!

There in the twilight cold and gray,
Lifeless, but beautiful, he lay,
And from the sky, serene and far,
A voice fell, like a falling star,
    Excelsior!

                H. W. LONGFELLOW.

THE BENDED BOW.

THERE was heard the sound of a coming foe,
There was sent through Britain a bended bow ;
And a voice was poured on the free winds far,
As the land rose up at the sign of war.

   "Heard you not the battle horn ?—
   Reaper! leave thy golden corn :
   Leave it for the birds of heaven—
   Swords must flash and spears be riven.
   Leave it for the winds to shed—
   Arm! ere Britain's turf grow red."
And the reaper armed, like a freeman's son ;
And the bended bow and the voice passed on.

" Hunter ! leave the mountain-chase,
Take the falchion from its place ;
Let the wolf go free to-day,
Leave him for a nobler prey ;
Let the deer ungalled sweep by—
Arm thee ! Britain's foes are nigh.".
And the hunter armed ere the chase was done ;
And the bended bow and the voice passed on.

" Chieftain ! quit the joyous feast—
Stay not till the song hath ceased :
Though the mead be foaming bright,
Though the fires give ruddy light,
Leave the hearth and leave the hall—
Arm thee ! Britain's foes must fall."
And the chieftain armed, and the horn was blown ;
And the bended bow and the voice passed on.

" Prince ! thy father's deeds are told
In the bower and the hold,
Where the goatherd's lay is sung,
Where the minstrel's harp is strung :
Foes are on thy native sea—
Give our bards a tale of thee ! "
And the prince came armed, like a leader's son ;
And the bended bow and the voice passed on.

" Mother ! stay thou not thy boy,
He must learn the battle's joy :
Sister ! bring the sword and spear,
Give thy brother words of cheer :
Maiden ! bid thy lover part :
Britain calls the strong in heart ! "
And the bended bow and the voice passed on ;
And the bards made song for a battle won.

                                        F. D. HEMANS.

THE FUGITIVES.

THE waters are flashing,
The white hail is dashing,
The lightnings are glancing,
The hoar-spray is dancing :—
     Away !

The whirlwind is rolling,
The thunder is tolling,
The forest is swinging,
The minster bells ringing :—
     Come away !

The earth is like ocean,
Wreck-strewn and in motion ;
Bird, beast, man, and worm,
Have crept out of the storm :—
     Come away !

"Our boat has one sail,
And the helmsman is pale.
A bold pilot, I trow,
Who should follow us now ! "
     Shouted he.

And she cried: " Ply the oar;
Put off gaily from shore ! "
As she spoke, bolts of death,
Mixed with hail, specked their path
     O'er the sea:

And from isle, tower, and rock,
The blue beacon-cloud broke:
And, though dumb in the blast,
The red cannon flashed fast
     From the lee.

And " Fear'st thou?" and " Fear'st thou?"
And " Seest thou?" and " Hear'st thou?"
And " Drive we not free
O'er the terrible sea,
      I and thou?"

One boat-cloak did cover
The loved and the lover:
Their blood beats one measure,
They murmur proud pleasure
      Soft and low;—

While around the lashed ocean,
Like mountains in motion,
Is withdrawn and uplifted,
Sunk, shattered, and shifted
      To and fro.

In the court of the fortress
Beside the pale portress,
Like a bloodhound well beaten
The bridegroom stands, eaten
      By shame.

On the topmost watch-turret,
As a death-boding spirit,
Stands the grey tyrant father;
To his voice the mad weather
      Seems tame;

And, with curses as wild
As e'er clung to child,
He devotes to the blast
The best, loveliest, and last,
      Of his name!

                    P. B. SHELLEY.

ON A DISTANT PROSPECT OF ETON COLLEGE.

Ye distant spires, ye antique towers,
  That crown the wat'ry glade,
Where grateful Science still adores
  Her Henry's holy shade;
And ye, that from the stately brow
Of Windsor's heights th' expanse below
  Of grove, of lawn, of mead survey,
Whose turf, whose shade, whose flowers among
Wanders the hoary Thames along
  His silver-winding way:

Ah, happy hills! ah, pleasing shade!
  Ah, fields belov'd in vain!
Where once my careless childhood stray'd,
  A stranger yet to pain!
I feel the gales that from ye blow
A momentary bliss bestow,
  As waving fresh their gladsome wing,
My weary soul they seem to soothe,
And, redolent of joy and youth,
  To breathe a second spring.

Say, Father Thames, for thou hast seen
  Full many a sprightly race
Disporting on thy margent green,
  The paths of pleasure trace;
Who foremost now delight to cleave,
With pliant arm, thy glassy wave?
  The captive linnet which enthrall?
What idle progeny succeed
To chase the rolling circle's speed,
  Or urge the flying ball?

While some on earnest business bent
  Their murm'ring labours ply
'Gainst graver hours that bring constraint
  To sweeten liberty:
Some bold adventurers disdain
The limits of their little reign,
  And unknown regions dare descry:
Still as they run they look behind,
They hear a voice in every wind,
  And snatch a fearful joy.

Gay hope is theirs by fancy fed,
  Less pleasing when possest;
The tear forgot as soon as shed,
  The sunshine of the breast:
Theirs buxom health, of rosy hue,
Wild wit, invention ever new,
  And lively cheer, of vigour born;
The thoughtless day, the easy night,
The spirits pure, the slumbers light,
  That fly th' approach of morn.

Alas! regardless of their doom
  The little victims play;
No sense have they of ills to come,
  No care beyond to-day:
Yet see, how all around 'em wait
The ministers of human fate,
  And black Misfortune's baleful train!
Ah, show them where in ambush stand,
To seize their prey, the murth'rous band!
  Ah, tell them, they are men!

These shall the fury Passions tear,
  The vultures of the mind,
Disdainful Anger, pallid Fear,
  And Shame that sculks behind;
Or pining Love shall waste their youth,
Or Jealousy, with rankling tooth,

That inly gnaws the secret heart ;
And Envy wan, and faded Care,
Grim-visag'd comfortless Despair,
　　And Sorrow's piercing dart.

Ambition this shall tempt to rise,
　　Then whirl the wretch from high,
To bitter Scorn a sacrifice,
　　And grinning Infamy.
The stings of Falsehood those shall try,
And hard Unkindness' alter'd eye,
　　That mocks the tear it forc'd to flow ;
And keen Remorse with blood defil'd,
And moody Madness laughing wild,
　　Amidst severest woe.

Lo ! in the vale of years beneath
　　A griesly troop are seen,
The painful family of Death,
　　More hideous than their queen :
This racks the joints, this fires the veins,
That every labouring sinew strains,
　　Those in the deeper vitals rage :
Lo ! Poverty, to fill the band,
That numbs the soul with icy hand,
　　And slow-consuming Age.

To each his suff'rings : all are men,
　　Condemn'd alike to groan ;
The tender for another's pain,
　　Th' unfeeling for his own.
Yet, ah ! why should they know their fate,
Since sorrow never comes too late,
　　And happiness too swiftly flies ?
Thought would destroy their paradise.
No more ;—where ignorance is bliss,
　　'Tis folly to be wise.
　　　　　　　　　　　　　T. GRAY.

WAR SONG

OF THE ROYAL EDINBURGH LIGHT DRAGOONS.

To horse! to horse! the standard flies,
  The bugles sound the call;
The Gallic navy stems the seas,
The voice of battle's on the breeze,
  Arouse ye, one and all!

From high Dunedin's towers we come,
  A band of brothers true;
Our casques the leopard's spoils surround,
With Scotland's hardy thistle crown'd;
  We boast the red and blue.

Though tamely crouch to Gallia's frown
  Dull Holland's tardy train;
Their ravish'd toys though Romans mourn.
Though gallant Switzers vainly spurn,
  And, foaming, gnaw the chain;

Oh! had they mark'd the avenging call
  Their brethren's murder gave,
Disunion ne'er their ranks had mown,
Nor patriot valour, desperate grown,
  Sought freedom in the grave!

Shall we, too, bend the stubborn head,
  In Freedom's temple born,
Dress our pale cheek in timid smile,
To hail a master in our isle,
  Or brook a victor's scorn?

No! though destruction o'er the land
  Come pouring as a flood,
The sun, that sees our falling day,
Shall mark our sabres' deadly sway,
  And set that night in blood.

For gold let Gallia's legions fight,
  Or plunder's bloody gain;
'Unbribed, unbought, our swords we draw,
To guard our king, to fence our law,
  Nor shall their edge be vain.

If ever breath of British gale
  Shall fan the tri-color,
Or footstep of invader rude,
With rapine foul, and red with blood,
  Pollute our happy shore,—

Then farewell home! and farewell friends!
  Adieu each tender tie!
Resolved, we mingle in the tide,
Where charging squadrons furious ride,
  To conquer or to die.

To horse! to horse! the sabres gleam;
  High sounds our bugle-call;
Combined by honour's sacred tie,
Our word is *Laws and Liberty!*
  March forward one and all!

Sir W. Scott.

THE LOSS OF THE   AL GEORGE.

Toll for the brave!
  The brave that ar   no more!
All sunk beneath the wave,
  Fast by their native shore!

Eight hundred of the brave,
  Whose courage well was tried,
Had made the vessel heel,
  And laid her on her side.

A land-breeze shook the shrouds,
    And she was overset;
Down went the Royal George,
    With all her crew complete.

Toll for the brave!
    Brave Kempenfelt is gone;
His last sea-fight is fought;
    His work of glory done.

It was not in the battle;
    No tempest gave the shock;
She sprang no fatal leak;
    She ran upon no rock.

His sword was in its sheath;
    His fingers held the pen,
When Kempenfelt went down
    With twice four hundred men.

Weigh the vessel up,
    Once dreaded by our foes!
And mingle with our cup
    The tear that England owes.

Her timbers yet are sound,
    d she may float again,
b   rged with England's thunder,
    and   the distant main.

But K   t is gone,
    His   are o'er;
And he and   is eight hundred
    Shall plough the wave no more.
                            W. COWPER.

SIR NICHOLAS AT MARSTON MOOR.

To horse, to horse, Sir Nicholas! the clarion's note is high;
To horse, to horse, Sir Nicholas! the huge drum makes
    reply:
Ere this hath Lucas marched with his gallant cavaliers,
And the bray of Rupert's trumpets grows fainter on our
    ears.
To horse, to horse, Sir Nicholas! White Guy is at the door,
And the vulture whets his beak o'er the field of Marston
    Moor.

Up rose the lady Alice from her brief and broken prayer,
And she brought a silken standard down the narrow
    turret stair.
Oh, many were the tears that those radiant eyes had shed,
As she worked the bright word "Glory" in the gay
    and glancing thread;
And mournful was the smile that o'er those beauteous
    features ran,
As she said, "It is your lady's gift, unfurl it in the van."

"It shall flutter, noble wench, where the best and boldest
    ride,
Through the steel-clad files of Skippon and the black
    dragoons of Pride;
The recreant soul of Fairfax will feel a sicklier qualm,
And the rebel lips of Oliver give out a louder psalm,
When they see my lady's gew-gaw flaunt bravely on their
    wing,
And hear her loyal soldiers' shout, for God and for the
    King!"—

'Tis noon; the ranks are broken along the royal line;
They fly, the braggarts of the Court, the bullies of the
    Rhine:
Stout Langley's cheer is heard no more, and Astley's helm
    is down,
And Rupert sheathes his rapier with a curse and with
    a frown;

G

And cold Newcastle mutters, as he follows in the flight,
" The German boar had better far have supped in York
    to-night."

The Knight is all alone, his steel cap cleft in twain,
His good buff jerkin crimsoned o'er with many a gory stain ;
But still he waves the standard, and cries amid the rout—
" For Church and King, fair gentlemen, spur on and fight
    it out ! "
And now he wards a Roundhead's pike, and now he
    hums a stave,
And here he quotes a stage-play, and there he fells a knave.

Good speed to thee, Sir Nicholas ! thou hast no thought
    of fear ;
Good speed to thee, Sir Nicholas ! but fearful odds are here.
The traitors ring thee round, and with every blow and
    thrust,
" Down, down," they cry, " with Belial, down with him
    to the dust ! "
" I would," quoth grim old Oliver, " that Belial's trusty
    sword
This day were doing battle for the Saints and for the
    Lord."—

The lady Alice sits with her maidens in her bower ;
The grey-haired warden watches on the castle's highest
    tower.—
" What news, what news, old Anthony ? "—" The field is
    lost and won ;
The ranks of war are melting as the mists beneath the
    sun ;
And a wounded man speeds hither,—I am told and cannot
    see,
Or sure I am that sturdy step my master's step should
    be."—

" I bring thee back the standard from as rude and rough
    a fray,
As e'er was proof of soldier's thews, or theme for minstrel's
    lay.

Bid Hubert fetch the silver bowl, and liquor *quantum suff.*;
I'll make a shift to drain it, ere I part with boot and buff;
Though Guy through many a gaping wound is breathing
    out his life,
And I come to thee a landless man, my fond and faithful
    wife!

"Sweet! we will fill our money-bags, and freight a ship
    for France,
And mourn in merry Paris for this poor realm's mis-
    chance;
Or, if the worst betide me, why, better axe or rope,
Than life with Lenthal for a king, and Peters for a pope!
Alas, alas, my gallant Guy!—out on the crop-eared boor,
That sent me with my standard on foot from Marston
    Moor!"

W. M. Praed.

THE INCHCAPE ROCK.

No stir in the air, no stir in the sea,
The ship was as still as she could be,
Her sails from heaven received no motion,
Her keel was steady in the ocean.

Without either sign or sound of their shock
The waves flow'd over the Inchcape Rock;
So little they rose, so little they fell,
They did not move the Inchcape Bell.

The Abbot of Aberbrothok
Had placed that bell on the Inchcape Rock;
On a buoy in the storm it floated and swung,
And over the waves its warning rung.

When the Rock was hid by the surge's swell,
The mariners heard the warning bell;
And then they knew the perilous Rock,
And blest the Abbot of Aberbrothok.

The Sun in heaven was shining gay,
All things were joyful on that day;
The sea birds scream'd as they wheel'd round,
And there was joyaunce in their sound.

The buoy of the Inchcape Bell was seen,
A darker speck on the ocean green;
Sir Ralph the Rover walk'd his deck,
And he fixed his eye on the darker speck.

He felt the cheering power of spring,
It made him whistle, it made him sing;
His heart was mirthful to excess,
But the Rover's mirth was wickedness.

His eye was on the Inchcape float;
Quoth he, "My men, put out the boat,
And row me to the Inchcape Rock,
And I'll plague the Abbot of Aberbrothok."

The boat is lower'd, the boatmen row,
And to the Inchcape Rock they go;
Sir Ralph bent over from the boat,
And he cut the Bell from the Inchcape float.

Down sunk the Bell with a gurgling sound,
The bubbles rose and burst around;
Quoth Sir Ralph, "The next who comes to the Rock
Won't bless the Abbot of Aberbrothok."

Sir Ralph the Rover sail'd away,
He scour'd the seas for many a day;
And now grown rich with plunder'd store,
He steers his course for Scotland's shore.

So thick a haze o'erspreads the sky,
They cannot see the Sun on high;
The wind hath blown a gale all day,
At evening it hath died away.

On the deck the Rover takes his stand,
So dark it is they see no land.
Quoth Sir Ralph, " It will be lighter soon,
For there is the dawn of the rising Moon."

" Canst hear," said one, " the breakers roar ?
For methinks we should be near the shore."
" Now where we are I cannot tell,
But I wish I could hear the Inchcape Bell."

They hear no sound, the swell is strong ;
Though the wind hath fallen they drift along,
Till the vessel strikes with a shivering shock,—
" Oh Christ ! it is the Inchcape Rock ! "

Sir Ralph the Rover tore his hair ;
He curst himself in his despair ;
The waves rush in on every side,
The ship is sinking beneath the tide.

But even in his dying fear
One dreadful sound could the Rover hear,
A sound as if with the Inchcape Bell,
The Devil below was ringing his knell.

R. SOUTHEY.

ELEGY WRITTEN IN A COUNTRY CHURCHYARD.

THE curfew tolls the knell of parting day,
  The lowing herd wind slowly o'er the lea,
The ploughman homeward plods his weary way,
  And leaves the world to darkness and to me.

Now fades the glimmering landscape on the sight,
  And all the air a solemn stillness holds,
Save where the beetle wheels his droning flight,
  And drowsy tinklings lull the distant folds :

Save that from yonder ivy-mantled tower,
    The moping owl does to the moon complain ,
Of such as, wand'ring near her sacred bower,
    Molest her ancient solitary reign.

Beneath those rugged elms, that yew-tree's shade,
    Where heaves the turf in many a mould'ring heap,
Each in his narrow cell for ever laid,
    The rude forefathers of the hamlet sleep.

The breezy call of incense-breathing morn,
    The swallow twittering from the straw-built shed,
The cock's shrill clarion, or the echoing horn,
    No more shall rouse them from their lowly bed.

For them no more the blazing hearth shall burn,
    Or busy housewife ply her evening care;
No children run to lisp their sire's return,
    Or climb his knees the envied kiss to share.

Oft did the harvest to their sickle yield,
    Their furrow oft the stubborn glebe has broke:
How jocund did they drive their team afield!
    How bow'd the woods beneath their sturdy stroke!

Let not ambition mock their useful toil,
    Their homely joys, and destiny obscure;
Nor grandeur hear with a disdainful smile
    The short and simple annals of the poor.

The boast of heraldry, the pomp of pow'r,
    And all that beauty, all that wealth e'er gave,
Await alike th' inevitable hour.
    The paths of glory lead but to the grave.

Nor you, ye proud, impute to these the fault,
    If memory o'er their tomb no trophies raise,
Wherethrough the long-drawn aisle and fretted vault
    The pealing anthem swells the note of praise.

Can storied urn, or animated bust,
  Back to its mansion call the fleeting breath?
Can honour's voice provoke the silent dust,
  Or flatt'ry soothe the dull cold ear of death?

Perhaps in this neglected spot is laid
  Some heart once pregnant with celestial fire;
Hands, that the rod of empire might have sway'd,
  Or wak'd to extasy the living lyre.

But knowledge to their eyes her ample page
  Rich with the spoils of time did ne'er unroll;
Chill penury repress'd their noble rage,
  And froze the genial current of the soul.

Full many a gem of purest ray serene
  The dark unfathom'd caves of ocean bear:
Full many a flower is born to blush unseen,
  And waste its sweetness on the desert air.

Some village Hampden, that, with dauntless breast,
  The little tyrant of his fields withstood,
Some mute inglorious Milton here may rest,
  Some Cromwell guiltless of his country's blood.

Th' applause of list'ning senates to command,
  The threats of pain and ruin to despise,
To scatter plenty o'er a smiling land,
  And read their history in a nation's eyes,

Their lot forbad: nor circumscrib'd alone
  Their growing virtues, but their crimes confin'd;
Forbad to wade through slaughter to a throne,
  And shut the gates of mercy on mankind,

The struggling pangs of conscious truth to hide,
  To quench the blushes of ingenuous shame,
Or heap the shrine of luxury and pride
  With incense kindled at the Muse's flame.

Far from the madding crowd's ignoble strife,
    Their sober wishes never learn'd to stray ;
Along the cool sequester'd vale of life
    They kept the noiseless tenor of their way.

Yet even these bones from insult to protect,
    Some frail memorial still erected nigh,
With uncouth rhymes and shapeless sculpture deck'd,
    Implores the passing tribute of a sigh.

Their name, their years, spelt by th' unletter'd Muse,
    The place of fame and elegy supply :
And many a holy text around she strews,
    That teach the rustic moralist to die.

For who, to dumb forgetfulness a prey,
    This pleasing anxious being e'er resign'd,
Left the warm precincts of the cheerful day,
    Nor cast one longing, ling'ring look behind ?

On some fond breast the parting soul relies,
    Some pious drops the closing eye requires ;
E'en from the tomb the voice of nature cries,
    E'en in our ashes live their wonted fires.

For thee, who, mindful of th' unhonour'd dead,
    Dost in these lines their artless tale relate ;
If chance, by lonely contemplation led,
    Some kindred spirit shall inquire thy fate,—

Haply some hoary-headed swain may say,
    "Oft have we seen him at the peep of dawn
Brushing with hasty steps the dews away,
    To meet the sun upon the upland lawn.

"There at the foot of yonder nodding beech,
    That wreathes its old fantastic roots so high,
His listless length at noontide would he stretch,
    And pore upon the brook that babbles by.

" Hard by yon wood, now smiling as in scorn,
  Mutt'ring his wayward fancies he would rove ;
Now drooping, woful-wan, like one forlorn,
  Or craz'd with care, or cross'd in hopeless love.

" One morn I miss'd him on the custom'd hill,
  Along the heath, and near his favourite tree ;
Another came ; nor yet beside the rill,
  Nor up the lawn, nor at the wood was he :

" The next, with dirges due in sad array
  Slow through the church-way path we saw him
    borne :—
Approach and read (for thou can'st read) the lay
  Grav'd on the stone beneath yon aged thorn."

THE EPITAPH.

Here rests his head upon the lap of earth
  A youth, to fortune and to fame unknown :
Fair science frown'd not on his humble birth,
  And melancholy mark'd him for her own.

Large was his bounty, and his soul sincere,
  Heaven did a recompense as largely send :
He gave to mis'ry (all he had) a tear,
  He gain'd from heav'n ('twas all he wish'd) a friend.

No farther seek his merits to disclose,
  Or draw his frailties from their dread abode,
(There they alike in trembling hope repose,)
  The bosom of his Father and his God.

                                    T. GRAY.

––––––•––––––

LORD ULLIN'S DAUGHTER.

A CHIEFTAIN, to the Highlands bound,
  Cries, " Boatman, do not tarry !
And I'll give thee a silver pound,
  To row us o'er the ferry."—

" Now who be ye, would cross Lochgyle,
    This dark and stormy water ? "—
" Oh ! I'm the chief of Ulva's isle,
    And this, Lord Ullin's daughter.

" And fast before her father's men
    Three days we've fled together,
For should he find us in the glen,
    My blood would stain the heather.

" His horsemen hard behind us ride;
    Should they our steps discover,
Then who will cheer my bonny bride,
    When they have slain her lover ? "—

Outspoke the hardy Highland wight,
    " I'll go, my chief—I'm ready :
It is not for your silver bright,
    But for your winsome lady :

" And by my word ! the bonny bird
    In danger shall not tarry ;
So, though the waves are raging white,
    I'll row you o'er the ferry."

By this the storm grew loud apace,
    The water-wraith was shrieking ;
And in the scowl of heaven each face
    Grew dark as they were speaking.

But still as wilder blew the wind,
    And as the night grew drearer,
Adown the glen rode armèd men,
    Their trampling sounded nearer.

" O haste thee, haste ! " the lady cries,
    " Though tempests round us gather ;
I'll meet the raging of the skies,
    But not an angry father."

The boat has left a stormy land,
　　A stormy sea before her,—
When, oh! too strong for human hand,
　　The tempest gathered o'er her.

And still they rowed amidst the roar
　　Of waters fast prevailing :
Lord Ullin reached that fatal shore,
　　His wrath was changed to wailing.

For, sore dismayed, through storm and shade,
　　His child he did discover ;
One lovely hand she stretched for aid,
　　And one was round her lover.

"Come back! come back!" he cried in grief,
　　"Across this stormy water ;
And I'll forgive your Highland chief,
　　My daughter! oh, my daughter!"

'Twas vain : the loud waves lashed the shore,
　　Return or aid preventing :
The waters wild went o'er his child,
　　And he was left lamenting.

T. CAMPBELL.

THE CLOUD.

I BRING fresh showers for the thirsting flowers
　　From the seas and the streams ;
I bear light shade for the leaves when laid
　　In their noonday dreams.
From my wings are shaken the dews that waken
　　The sweet buds every one,
When rocked to rest on their Mother's breast,
　　As she dances about the sun.
I wield the flail of the lashing hail,
　　And whiten the green plains under ;
And then again I dissolve it in rain,
　　And laugh as I pass in thunder.

I sift the snow on the mountains below,
    And their great pines groan aghast;
And all the night 'tis my pillow white,
    While I sleep in the arms of the Blast.
Sublime on the towers of my skiey bowers
    Lightning my pilot sits;
In a cavern under is fettered the Thunder,
    It struggles and howls at fits.
Over earth and ocean with gentle motion
    This pilot is guiding me,
Lured by the love of the Genii that move
    In the depths of the purple sea;
Over the rills and the crags and the hills,
    Over the lakes and the plains,
Wherever he dream under mountain or stream
    The Spirit he loves remains;
And I all the while bask in heaven's blue smile,
    Whilst he is dissolving in rains.

The sanguine Sunrise, with his meteor eyes,
    And his burning plumes outspread,
Leaps on the back of my sailing rack,
    When the morning star shines dead:
As on the jag of a mountain crag
    Which an earthquake rocks and swings
An eagle alit one moment may sit
    In the light of its golden wings.
And, when Sunset may breathe, from the lit sea beneath,
    Its ardours of rest and of love,
And the crimson pall of eve may fall
    From the depth of heaven above,
With wings folded I rest on mine airy nest,
    As still as a brooding dove.

That orbèd maiden with white fire laden
    Whom mortals call the Moon
Glides glimmering o'er my fleece-like floor
    By the midnight breezes strewn;
And wherever the beat of her unseen feet,
    Which only the angels hear,

May have broken the woof of my tent's thin roof,
    The Stars peep behind her and peer.
And I laugh to see them whirl and flee
    Like a swarm of golden bees,
When I widen the rent in my wind-built tent,—
    Till the calm rivers, lakes, and seas,
Like strips of the sky fallen through me on high,
    Are each paved with the moon and these.

I bind the Sun's throne with a burning zone,
    And the Moon's with a girdle of pearl;
The volcanoes are dim, and the Stars reel and swim,
    When the Whirlwinds my banner unfurl.
From cape to cape, with a bridge-like shape,
    Over a torrent sea,
Sunbeam-proof, I hang like a roof;
    The mountains its columns be.
The triumphal arch through which I march,
    With hurricane, fire, and snow,
When the Powers of the air are chained to my chair,
    Is the million-coloured bow;
The Sphere-fire above its soft colours wove,
    While the moist Earth was laughing below.

I am the daughter of Earth and Water,
    And the nursling of the Sky:
I pass through the pores of the ocean and shores;
    I change, but I cannot die.
For after the rain, when with never a stain
    The pavilion of heaven is bare,
And the winds and sunbeams with their convex gleams
    Build up the blue dome of air,
I silently laugh at my own cenotaph,—
    And out of the caverns of rain,
Like a child from the womb, like a ghost from the tomb,
    I arise, and unbuild it again.

                        P. B. SHELLEY.

MY PSALM.

I MOURN no more my vanished years:
　Beneath a tender rain,
An April rain of smiles and tears,
　My heart is young again.

The west-winds blow, and, singing low,
　I hear the glad streams run;
The windows of my soul I throw
　Wide open to the sun.

No longer forward nor behind
　I look in hope or fear;
But, grateful, take the good I find,
　The best of now and here.

I plough no more a desert land,
　To harvest weed and tare;
The manna dropping from God's hand
　Rebukes my painful care.

I break my pilgrim staff,—I lay
　Aside the toiling oar;
The angel sought so far away
　I welcome at my door.

The airs of spring may never play
　Among the ripening corn,
Nor freshness of the flowers of May
　Blow through the autumn morn;

Yet shall the blue-eyed gentian look
　Through fringèd lids to heaven,
And the pale aster in the brook
　Shall see its image given;—

The woods shall wear their robes of praise,
  The south-wind softly sigh,
And sweet, calm days in golden haze
  Melt down the amber sky.

Not less shall manly deed and word
  Rebuke an age of wrong;
The graven flowers that wreathe the sword
  Make not the blade less strong.

But smiting hands shall learn to heal,—
  To build as to destroy;
Nor less my heart for others feel
  That I the more enjoy.

All as God wills, who wisely heeds
  To give or to withhold,
And knoweth more of all my needs
  Than all my prayers have told!

Enough that blessings undeserved
  Have marked my erring track;—
That wheresoe'er my feet have swerved,
  His chastening turned me back;—

That more and more a Providence
  Of love is understood,
Making the springs of time and sense
  Sweet with eternal good;—

That death seems but a covered way
  Which opens into light,
Wherein no blinded child can stray
  Beyond the Father's sight;—

That care and trial seem at last,
  Through Memory's sunset air,
Like mountain-ranges overpast,
  In purple distance fair;—

That all the jarring notes of life
　Seem blending in a psalm,
And all the angles of its strife
　Slow rounding into calm.

And so the shadows fall apart,
　And so the west-winds play;
And all the windows of my heart
　I open to the day.

J. G. WHITTIER.

THE SPANISH ARMADA.

ATTEND, all ye who list to hear our noble England's praise;
I tell of the thrice famous deeds she wrought in ancient
　　days,
When that great fleet invincible against her bore in vain
The richest spoils of Mexico, the stoutest hearts of Spain.

It was about the lovely close of a warm summer day,
There came a gallant merchant-ship full sail to Plymouth
　　Bay;
Her crew hath seen Castile's black fleet, beyond Aurigny's
　　isle,
At earliest twilight, on the waves lie heaving many a
　　mile.
At sunrise she escaped their van, by God's especial grace
And the tall Pinta, till the noon, had held her close in
　　chase.
Forthwith a guard at every gun was placed along the
　　wall;
The beacon blazed upon the roof of Edgecumbe's lofty
　　hall;
Many a light fishing-bark put out to pry along the coast,
And with loose rein and bloody spur rode inland many a
　　post.

With his white hair unbonnetted, the stout old sheriff
comes;
Behind him march the halberdiers; before him sound the
drums;
His yeomen round the market cross make clear an ample
space;
For there behoves him to set up the standard of Her Grace.
And haughtily the trumpets peal, and gaily dance the
bells,
As slow upon the labouring wind the royal blazon swells.
Look how the Lion of the sea lifts up his ancient crown,
And underneath his deadly paw treads the gay lilies
down.
So stalk'd he when he turned to flight, on that famed
Picard field,
Bohemia's plume, and Genoa's bow, and Cæsar's eagle
shield.
So glared he when at Agincourt in wrath he turned to
bay,
And crushed and torn beneath his claws the princely
hunters lay.
Ho! strike the flagstaff deep, Sir Knight: ho! scatter
flowers, fair maids:
Ho! gunners, fire a loud salute: ho! gallants, draw your
blades:
Thou sun, shine on her joyously; ye breezes, waft her
wide;
Our glorious *SEMPER EADEM*, the banner of our pride.

The freshening breeze of eve unfurled that banner's
massy fold;
The parting gleam of sunshine kissed that haughty scroll
of gold;
Night sank upon the dusky beach, and on the purple sea,
Such night in England ne'er had been, nor e'er again
shall be.
From Eddystone to Berwick bounds, from Lynn to Mil-
ford Bay,
That time of slumber was as bright and busy as the day;

H

For swift to east and swift to west the ghastly war-flame
  spread,
High on St. Michael's Mount it shone : it shone on Beachy
  Head.
Far on the deep the Spaniard saw, along each southern
  shire,
Cape beyond cape, in endless range, those twinkling points
  of fire.
The fisher left his skiff to rock on Tamar's glittering
  waves :
The rugged miners poured to war from Mendip's sunless
  caves :
O'er Longleat's towers, o'er Cranbourne's oaks, the fiery
  herald flew :
He roused the shepherds of Stonehenge, the rangers of
  Beaulieu.
Right sharp and quick the bells all night rang out from
  Bristol town,
And ere the day three hundred horse had met on Clifton
  down ;
The sentinel on Whitehall gate looked forth into the
  night,
And saw o'erhanging Richmond Hill the streak of blood-
  red light.
Then bugle's note and cannon's roar the deathlike silence
  broke,
And with one start, and with one cry, the royal city
  woke.
At once on all her stately gates arose the answering fires ;
At once the wild alarum clashed from all her reeling
  spires ;
From all the batteries of the Tower pealed loud the voice
  of fear ;
And all the thousand masts of Thames sent back a louder
  cheer :
And from the furthest wards was heard the rush of
  hurrying feet,
And the broad streams of pikes and flags rushed down
  each roaring street ;
And broader still became the blaze, and louder still the
  din,

As fast from every village round the horse came spurring
in :
And eastward straight from wild Blackheath the warlike
errand went,
And roused in many an ancient hall the gallant squires
of Kent.
Southward from Surrey's pleasant hills flew those bright
couriers forth ;
High on bleak Hampstead's swarthy moor they started
for the north ;
And on, and on, without a pause, untired they bounded
still :
All night from tower to tower they sprang ; they sprang
from hill to hill :
Till the proud peak unfurled the flag o'er Darwin's rocky
dales,
Till like volcanoes flared to heaven the stormy hills of
Wales,
Till twelve fair counties saw the blaze on Malvern's lonely
height,
Till streamed in crimson on the wind the Wrekin's crest
of light,
Till broad and fierce the star came forth on Ely's stately
fane,
And tower and hamlet rose in arms o'er all the boundless
plain ;
Till Belvoir's lordly terraces the sign to Lincoln sent,
And Lincoln sped the message on o'er the wide vale of
Trent ;
Till Skiddaw saw the fire that burned on Gaunt's embattled
pile,
And the red glare on Skiddaw roused the burghers of
Carlisle.

LORD MACAULAY.

THE BATTLE AUTUMN OF 1862.

THE flags of war like storm-birds fly,
  The charging trumpets blow;
Yet rolls no thunder in the sky,
  No earthquake strives below.

And, calm and patient, Nature keeps
  Her ancient promise well,
Though o'er her bloom and greenness sweeps
  The battle's breath of hell.

And still she walks in golden hours
  Through harvest-happy farms,
And still she wears her fruits and flowers
  Like jewels on her arms.

What mean the gladness of the plain,
  This joy of eve and morn,
The mirth that shakes the beard of grain
  And yellow locks of corn?

Ah! eyes may well be full of tears,
  And hearts with hate are hot;
But even-paced come round the years,
  And Nature changes not.

She meets with smiles our bitter grief,
  With songs our groans of pain;
She mocks with tint of flower and leaf
  The war-field's crimson stain.

Still, in the cannon's pause, we hear
  Her sweet thanksgiving-psalm;
Too near to God for doubt or fear,
  She shares the eternal calm.

She knows the seed lies safe below
  The fires that blast and burn ;
For all the tears of blood we sow
  She waits the rich return.

She sees with clearer eye than ours
  The good of suffering born,—
The hearts that blossom like her flowers,
  And ripen like her corn.

O, give to us, in times like these,
  The vision of her eyes ;
And make her fields and fruited trees
  Our golden prophecies !

O, give to us her finer ear !
  Above this stormy din,
We too would hear the bells of cheer
  Ring peace and freedom in !

J. G. WHITTIER.

THE VILLAGE BLACKSMITH.

UNDER a spreading chestnut-tree
  The village smithy stands ;
The smith, a mighty man is he,
  With large and sinewy hands ;
And the muscles of his brawny arms
  Are strong as iron bands.

His hair is crisp, and black, and long,
  His face is like the tan ;
His brow is wet with honest sweat,
  He earns whate'er he can,
And looks the whole world in the face,
  For he owes not any man.

Week in, week out, from morn till night,
  You can hear his bellows blow;
You can hear him swing his heavy sledge
  With measured beat and slow,
Like a sexton ringing the village bell,
  When the evening sun is low.

And children coming home from school
  Look in at the open door;
They love to see the flaming forge,
  And hear the bellows roar,
And catch the burning sparks that fly
  Like chaff from a threshing-floor.

He goes on Sunday to the church,
  And sits among his boys;
He hears the parson pray and preach,
  He hears his daughter's voice
Singing in the village choir,
  And makes his heart rejoice.

It sounds to him like her mother's voice,
  Singing in Paradise!
He needs must think of her once more,
  How in the grave she lies;
And with his hard, rough hand he wipes
  A tear out of his eyes.

Toiling,—rejoicing,—sorrowing,
  Onward through life he goes;
Each morning sees some task begun,
  Each evening sees it close;
Something attempted, something done,
  Has earned a night's repose.

Thanks, thanks to thee, my worthy friend,
  For the lesson thou hast taught!
Thus at the flaming forge of life
  Our fortunes must be wrought;
Thus on its sounding anvil shaped
  Each burning deed and thought.
                              H. W. LONGFELLOW.

THE BELLS.

Hear the sledges with the bells
Silver bells!
What a world of merriment their melody foretells!
How they tinkle, tinkle, tinkle,
In the icy air of night!
While the stars that oversprinkle
All the heavens seem to twinkle
With a crystalline delight;
Keeping time, time, time,
In a sort of Runic rhyme,
To the tintinnabulation that so musically wells
From the bells, bells, bells, bells,
Bells, bells, bells—
From the jingling and the tinkling of the bells.

Hear the mellow wedding bells,
Golden bells!
What a world of happiness their harmony foretells!
Through the balmy air of night
How they ring out their delight!
From the molten-golden notes,
And all in tune,
What a liquid ditty floats
To the turtle-dove that listens, while she gloats
On the moon!
Oh, from out the sounding cells,
What a gush of euphony voluminously wells!
How it swells!
How it dwells
On the Future! how it tells
Of the rapture that impels
To the swinging and the ringing
Of the bells, bells, bells,
Of the bells, bells, bells, bells,
Bells, bells, bells—
To the rhyming and the chiming of the bells!

Hear the loud alarum bells—
Brazen bells!
What a tale of terror, now, their turbulency tells!
In the startled ear of night
How they scream out their affright!
Too much horrified to speak,
They can only shriek, shriek,
Out of tune,
In a clamorous appealing to the mercy of the fire,
In a mad expostulation with the deaf and frantic fire
Leaping higher, higher, higher,
With a desperate desire,
And a resolute endeavour
Now—now to sit or never,
By the side of the pale-faced moon.
Oh, the bells, bells, bells!
What a tale their terror tells
Of Despair!
How they clang, and clash, and roar!
What a horror they outpour
On the bosom of the palpitating air!
Yet the ear it fully knows,
By the twanging,
And the clanging,
How the danger ebbs and flows;
Yet the ear distinctly tells,
In the jangling,
And the wrangling,
How the danger sinks and swells,
By the sinking or the swelling in the anger of the bells—
Of the bells—
Of the bells, bells, bells, bells,
Bells, bells, bells—
In the clamour and the clangour of the bells!

Hear the tolling of the bells—
Iron bells!
What a world of solemn thought their monody compels!
In the silence of the night
How we shiver with affright

At the melancholy menace of their tone!
　　For every sound that floats
　　From the rust within their throats
　　　　Is a groan.
　　And the people—ah, the people—
　　They that dwell up in the steeple,
　　　　All alone,
　　And who, tolling, tolling, tolling,
　　　In that muffled monotone,
　　Feel a glory in so rolling
　　　On the human heart a stone—
They are neither man nor woman—
They are neither brute nor human—
　　　　They are Ghouls:
　　And their king it is who tolls;
　　And he rolls, rolls, rolls,
　　　　Rolls
　　A pæan from the bells!
　　And his merry bosom swells
　　　With the pæan of the bells!
　　And he dances, and he yells;
　　Keeping time, time, time,
　　In a sort of Runic rhyme,
　　　To the pæan of the bells!
　　　Of the bells!
　　Keeping time, time, time,
　　In a sort of Runic rhyme,
　　　To the throbbing of the bells—
　　Of the bells, bells, bells—
　　　To the sobbing of the bells;
　　Keeping time, time, time,
　　　As he knells, knells, knells,
　　In a happy Runic rhyme,
　　　To the rolling of the bells—
　　Of the bells, bells, bells—
　　　To the tolling of the bells,
　　Of the bells, bells, bells, bells—
　　　　Bells, bells, bells—
To the moaning and the groaning of the bells.

E. A. POE.

TO A SKYLARK.

HAIL to thee, blithe spirit—
Bird thou never wert—
That from heaven or near it
Pourest thy full heart
In profuse strains of unpremeditated art.

Higher still and higher
From the earth thou springest :
Like a cloud of fire,
The blue deep thou wingest,
And singing still dost soar, and soaring ever singest.

In the golden lightning
Of the sunken sun,
O'er which clouds are brightening,
Thou dost float and run,
Like an embodied joy whose race is just begun.

The pale purple even
Melts around thy flight ;
Like a star of heaven
In the broad daylight,
Thou art unseen, but yet I hear thy shrill delight—

Keen as are the arrows
Of that silver sphere
Whose intense lamp narrows
In the white dawn clear,
Until we hardly see, we feel, that it is there.

All the earth and air
With thy voice is loud,
As, when night is bare,
From one lonely cloud
The moon rains out her beams, and heaven is overflowed.

What, thou art we know not;
    What is most like thee?
From rainbow clouds there flow not
    Drops so bright to see
As from thy presence showers a rain of melody :—

Like a poet hidden
    In the light of thought,
Singing hymns unbidden,
    Till the world is wrought
To sympathy with hopes and fears it heeded not :

Like a high-born maiden
    In a palace tower,
Soothing her love-laden
    Soul in secret hour
With music sweet as love which overflows her bower

Like a glow-worm golden
    In a dell of dew,
Scattering unbeholden
    Its aërial hue
Among the flowers and grass which screen it from the view :

Like a rose embowered
    In its own green leaves,
By warm winds deflowered,
    Till the scent it gives
Makes faint with too much sweet these heavy-wingèd
    thieves.

Sound of vernal showers
    On the twinkling grass,
Rain-awakened flowers,—
    All that ever was,
Joyous and clear and fresh,—thy music doth surpass.

Teach us, sprite or bird,
    What sweet thoughts are thine :
I have never heard
    Praise of love or wine
That panted forth a flood of rapture so divine.

Chorus hymeneal
  Or triumphal chant,
Matched with thine, would be all
  But an empty vaunt—
A thing wherein we feel there is some hidden want.

What objects are the fountains
  Of thy happy strain?
What fields, or waves, or mountains?
  What shapes of sky or plain?
What love of thine own kind? what ignorance of pain?

With thy clear keen joyance
  Languor cannot be:
Shadow of annoyance
  Never came near thee:
Thou lovest, but ne'er knew love's sad satiety.

Waking or asleep,
  Thou of death must deem
Things more true and deep
  Than we mortals dream,
Or how could thy notes flow in such a crystal stream?

We look before and after,
  And pine for what is not:
Our sincerest laughter
  With some pain is fraught;
Our sweetest songs are those that tell of saddest thought.

Yet, if we could scorn
  Hate and pride and fear,
If we were things born
  Not to shed a tear,
I know not how thy joy we ever should come near.

Better than all measures
  Of delightful sound,
Better than all treasures
  That in books are found,
Thy skill to poet were, thou scorner of the ground!

Teach me half the gladness
That thy brain must know;
Such harmonious madness
From my lips would flow,
The world should listen then as I am listening now.

P. B. SHELLEY.

DEATH'S FINAL CONQUEST.

THE glories of our blood and state
    Are shadows, not substantial things;
There is no armour against fate;
    Death lays his icy hand on kings:
        Sceptre and crown
        Must tumble down,
And in the dust be equal made
With the poor crookèd scythe and spade.

Some men with swords may reap the field,
    And plant fresh laurels where they kill;
But their strong nerves at last must yield;
    They tame but one another still:
        Early or late,
        They stoop to fate,
And must give up their murmuring breath,
When they, pale captives, creep to death.

The garlands wither on your brow,
    Then boast no more your mighty deeds;
Upon Death's purple altar now,
    See, where the victor-victim bleeds.
        Your heads must come
        To the cold tomb,
Only the actions of the just
Smell sweet, and blossom in their dust.

J. SHIRLEY.

HOW THEY BROUGHT THE GOOD NEWS FROM GHENT TO AIX.

I SPRANG to the stirrup, and Joris, and he;
I galloped, Dirck galloped, we galloped all three;
" Good speed ! " cried the watch, as the gate-bolts undrew ;
" Speed ! " echoed the wall to us galloping through ;
Behind shut the postern, the lights sank to rest,
And into the midnight we galloped abreast.

Not a word to each other; we kept the great pace
Neck by neck, stride by stride, never changing our place;
I turned in my saddle and made its girths tight,
Then shortened each stirrup, and set the pique right,
Rebuckled the cheek-strap, chained slacker the bit,
Nor galloped less steadily Roland a whit.

'Twas moonset at starting ; but while we drew near
Lokeren, the cocks crew and twilight dawned clear ;
At Boom, a great yellow star came out to see ;
At Düffeld, 'twas morning as plain as could be ;
And from Mecheln church-steeple we heard the half chime
So Joris broke silence with, " Yet there is time ! "

At Aerschot, up leaped of a sudden the sun,
And against him the cattle stood black every one,
To stare thro' the mist at us galloping past,
And I saw my stout galloper Roland at last,
With resolute shoulders, each butting away
The haze, as some bluff river headland its spray.

And his low head and crest, just one sharp ear bent back
For my voice, and the other pricked out on his track ;
And one eye's black intelligence,—ever that glance
O'er its white edge at me, his own master, askance !
And the thick heavy spume-flakes which aye and anon
His fierce lips shook upwards in galloping on.

By Hasselt, Dirck groaned; and cried Joris, " Stay spur !
" Your Roos galloped bravely, the fault's not in her,
" We'll remember at Aix"—for one heard the quick wheeze
Of her chest, saw the stretched neck and staggering knees,
And sunk tail, and horrible heave of the flank,
As down on her haunches she shuddered and sank.

So we were left galloping, Joris and I,
Past Loos, and past Tongres, no cloud in the sky ;
The broad sun above laughed a pitiless laugh,
'Neath our feet broke the brittle bright stubble like chaff ;
Till over by Dalhem a dome-spire sprang white,
And " Gallop," cried Joris, " for Aix is in sight ! "

" How they'll greet us ! "—and all in a moment his roan
Rolled neck and croup over, lay dead as a stone ;
And there was my Roland to bear the whole weight
Of the news which alone could save Aix from her fate,
With his nostrils like pits full of blood to the brim,
And with circles of red for his eye-sockets' rim.

Then I cast loose my buffcoat, each holster let fall,
Shook off both my jack-boots, let go belt and all,
Stood up in the stirrup, leaned, patted his ear,
Called my Roland his pet-name, my horse without peer ;
Clapped my hands, laughed and sang, any noise, bad or good,
Till at length into Aix Roland galloped and stood.

And all I remember is, friends flocking round
As I sate with his head 'twixt my knees on the ground,
And no voice but was praising this Roland of mine,
As I poured down his throat our last measure of wine,
Which (the burgesses voted by common consent)
Was no more than his due who brought good news from
    Ghent.

R. BROWNING.

THE BATTLE OF BLENHEIM.

Iᴛ was a summer evening,
  Old Kaspar's work was done,
And he before his cottage door
  Was sitting in the sun,
And by him sported on the green
His little grandchild Wilhelmine.

She saw her brother Peterkin
  Roll something large and round,
Which he beside the rivulet
  In playing there had found;
He came to ask what he had found,
That was so large, and smooth, and round.

Old Kaspar took it from the boy,
  Who stood expectant by;
And then the old man shook his head,
  And with a natural sigh,
" 'Tis some poor fellow's skull," said he
" Who fell in the great victory.

" I find them in the garden,
  For there's many here about;
And often, when I go to plough,
  The ploughshare turns them out!
For many a thousand men," said he,
" Were slain in that great victory."

" Now tell us what 'twas all about,"
  Young Peterkin, he cries;
And little Wilhelmine looks up
  With wonder-waiting eyes;
" Now tell us all about the war   ...d anon
And what they fought each other f(

" It was the English," Kaspar cried,
  " Who put the French to rout ;
But what they fought each other for.
  I could not well make out ;
But everybody said," quoth he,
" That 'twas a famous victory.

" My father lived at Blenheim then,
  Yon little stream hard by ;
They burnt his dwelling to the ground,
  And he was forced to fly ;
So with his wife and child he fled,
Nor had he where to rest his head.

" With fire and sword the country round
  Was wasted far and wide,
And many a childing mother then,
  And new-born baby died ;
But things like that, you know, must be
At every famous victory.

" They say it was a shocking sight
  After the field was won ;
For many thousand bodies here
  Lay rotting in the sun ;
But things like that, you know, must be
After a famous victory.

" Great praise the Duke of Marlbro' won,
  And our good Prince Eugene."
" Why 'twas a very wicked thing ! "
  Said little Wilhelmine.
 'Nay .. nay .. my little girl," quoth he,
" It was a famous victory.

" And everybody praised the Duke,
  Who such a fight did win."
" But what good came of it at last ? "
  Quoth little Peterkin.
" Why that I cannot tell," said he,
" But 'twas a famous victory."

                    R. SOUTHEY.

I

THE ENGLISH BOY.

Look from the ancient mountains down,
   My noble English boy!
Thy country's fields around thee gleam
   In sunlight and in joy.

Ages have rolled since foeman's march
   Passed o'er that old firm sod;
For well the land hath fealty held
   To freedom and to God!

Gaze proudly on, my English boy!
   And let thy kindling mind
Drink in the spirit of high thought
   From every chainless wind.

There, in the shadow of old Time,
   The halls beneath thee lie
Which poured forth to the fields of yore
   Our England's chivalry.

How bravely and how solemnly
   They stand, midst oak and yew,
Whence Cressy's yeomen haply framed
   The bow, in battle true;

And round their walls the good swords hang
   Whose faith knew no alloy,
And shields of knighthood, pure from stain.
   Gaze on, my English boy!

Gaze where the hamlet's ivied church
   Gleams by the antique elm,
Or where the minster lifts the cross
   High through the air's blue realm.

Martyrs have showered their free heart's blood
  That England's prayer might rise,
From those gray fanes of thoughtful years,
  Unfettered to the skies.

Along their aisles, beneath their trees,
  This earth's most glorious dust,
Once fired with valour, wisdom, song,
  Is laid in holy trust.

Gaze on—gaze farther, farther yet—
  My gallant English boy !
Yon blue sea bears thy country's flag,
  The billow's pride and joy.

Those waves in many a fight have closed
  Above her faithful dead ;
That red-cross flag victoriously
  Hath floated o'er their bed.

They perished—this green turf to keep
  By hostile tread unstained,
These knightly halls inviolate,
  Those churches unprofaned.

And high and clear their memory's light
  Along our shore is set,
And many an answering beacon-fire
  Shall there be kindled yet.

Lift up thy heart, my English boy !
  And pray, like them to stand,
Should God so summon thee, to guard
  The altars of the land.

F. D. HEMANS.

IVRY.

Now glory to the Lord of Hosts, from whom all glories
    are!
And glory to our Sovereign Liege, King Henry of Navarre!
Now let there be the merry sound of music and of dance,
Through thy corn-fields green, and sunny vines, oh plea-
    sant land of France!
And thou, Rochelle, our own Rochelle, proud city of the
    waters,
Again let rapture light the eyes of all thy mourning
    daughters.
As thou wert constant in our ills, be joyous in our joy,
For cold, and stiff, and still are they who wrought thy
    walls annoy.
Hurrah! Hurrah! a single field hath turned the chance
    of war,
Hurrah! Hurrah! for Ivry, and Henry of Navarre.

Oh! how our hearts were beating, when, at the dawn of
    day,
We saw the army of the League drawn out in long array;
With all its priest-led citizens, and all its rebel peers,
And Appenzel's stout infantry, and Egmont's Flemish
    spears.
There rode the brood of false Lorraine, the curses of our
    land;
And dark Mayenne was in the midst, a truncheon in his
    hand:
And, as we looked on them, we thought of Seine's em-
    purpled flood,
And good Coligni's hoary hair all dabbled with his blood;
And we cried unto the living God, who rules the fate of
    war,
To fight for His own holy name, and Henry of Navarre.

The King is come to marshal us, in all his armour drest,
And he has bound a snow-white plume upon his gallant
    crest.

He looked upon his people, and a tear was in his eye ;
He looked upon the traitors, and his glance was stern and
    high.
Right graciously he smiled on us, as rolled from wing to
    wing,
Down all our line, a deafening shout, " God save our Lord
    the King ! "
" And if my standard-bearer fall, as fall full well he may,
For never saw I promise yet of such a bloody fray,
Press where ye see my white plume shine, amidst the
    ranks of war,
And be your oriflamme to-day the helmet of Navarre."

Hurrah ! the foes are moving. Hark to the mingled din
Of fife, and steed, and trump, and drum, and roaring
    culverin.
The fiery Duke is pricking fast across Saint André's plain,
With all the hireling chivalry of Guelders and Almayne.
Now by the lips of those ye love, fair gentlemen of France,
Charge for the golden lilies,—upon them with the lance.
A thousand spurs are striking deep, a thousand spears in
    rest,
A thousand knights are pressing close behind the snow-
    white crest ;
And in they burst, and on they rushed, while, like a
    guiding star,
Amidst the thickest carnage blazed the helmet of Navarre.

Now, God be praised, the day is ours. Mayenne hath
    turned his rein.
D'Aumale hath cried for quarter. The Flemish count is
    slain.
Their ranks are breaking like thin clouds before a Biscay
    gale ;
The field is heaped with bleeding steeds, and flags, and
    cloven mail.
And then we thought on vengeance, and, all along our
    van,
" Remember Saint Bartholomew," was passed from man
    to man.

But out spake gentle Henry, " No Frenchman is my foe :
Down, down with every foreigner, but let your brethren
        go."
Oh! was there ever such a knight, in friendship or in war,
As our Sovereign Lord, King Henry, the soldier of Navarre?

Right well fought all the Frenchmen who fought for
        France to-day,
And many a lordly banner God gave them for a prey.
But we of the religion have borne us best in fight ;
And the good Lord of Rosny has ta'en the cornet white.
Our own true Maximilian the cornet white hath ta'en,
The cornet white with crosses black, the flag of false
        Lorraine.
Up with it high; unfurl it wide; that all the host may know
How God hath humbled the proud house which wrought
        His church such woe.
Then on the ground, while trumpets sound their loudest
        point of war,
Fling the red shreds, a footcloth meet for Henry of
        Navarre.

Ho! maidens of Vienna ; Ho! matrons of Lucerne ;
Weep, weep, and rend your hair for those who never shall
        return.
Ho! Philip, send, for charity, thy Mexican pistoles,
That Antwerp monks may sing a mass for thy poor spear-
        men's souls.
Ho! gallant nobles of the League, look that your arms be
        bright ;
Ho! burghers of Saint Genevieve, keep watch and ward
        to-night,
For our God hath crushed the tyrant, our God hath raised
        the slave,
And mocked the counsel of the wise, and the valour of the
        brave.
Then glory to His holy name, from whom all glories are ;
And glory to our Sovereign Lord, King Henry of Navarre.
                                LORD MACAULAY.

BATTLE OF THE BALTIC.

Of Nelson and the North,
Sing the glorious day's renown,
When to battle fierce came forth
All the might of Denmark's crown,
And her arms along the deep proudly shone;
By each gun the lighted brand,
In a bold determined hand,
And the Prince of all the land
Led them on.—

Like leviathans afloat,
Lay their bulwarks on the brine;
While the sign of battle flew
On the lofty British line:
It was ten of April morn by the chime:
As they drifted on their path,
There was silence deep as death;
And the boldest held his breath,
For a time.—

But the might of England flush'd
To anticipate the scene;
And her van the fleeter rush'd
O'er the deadly space between.
" Hearts of oak ! " our captains cried; when each gun
From its adamantine lips
Spread a death-shade round the ships,
Like the hurricane eclipse
Of the sun.—

Again! again; again!
And the havoc did not slack,
Till a feeble cheer the Dane
To our cheering, sent us back;—

Their shots along the deep slowly.boom :—
Then ceased—and all is wail,
As they strike the shatter'd sail ;
Or, in conflagration pale,
Light the gloom.—

Out spoke the victor then,
As he hail'd them o'er the wave,
" Ye are brothers ! ye are men !
And we conquer but to save :
So peace instead of death let us bring ;
But yield, proud foe, thy fleet,
With the crews, at England's feet,
And make submission meet
To our King."—

Then Denmark bless'd our chief,
That he gave her wounds repose ;
And the sounds of joy and grief
From her people wildly rose,
As death withdrew his shades from the day.
While the sun looked smiling bright
O'er a wide and woeful sight,
Where the fires of funeral light
Died away.—

Now joy, old England, raise !
For the tidings of thy might,
By the festal cities' blaze,
Whilst the wine cup shines in light ;
And yet amidst that joy and uproar,
Let us think of them that sleep,
Full many a fathom deep,
By thy wild and stormy steep,
Elsinore !—

Brave hearts ! to Britain's pride
Once so faithful and so true,
On the deck of fame that died,—
With the gallant good Riou : *

* Captain Riou, justly entitled the gallant and the good by Lord Nelson, in his dispatches.

Soft sigh the winds of heaven o'er their grave !
While the billow mournful rolls,
And the mermaid's song condoles,
Singing glory to the souls
Of the brave !—

T. CAMPBELL.

———•———

BALLAD OF ROSABELLE.

O, LISTEN, listen, ladies gay !
    No haughty feat of arms I tell ;
Soft is the note, and sad the lay,
    That mourns the lovely Rosabelle.

—" Moor, moor the barge, ye gallant crew !
    And, gentle ladye, deign to stay !
Rest thee in Castle Ravensheuch,
    Nor tempt the stormy firth to-day.

" The blackening wave is edged with white ;
    To inch * and rock the sea-mews fly ;
The fishers have heard the Water-Sprite,
    Whose screams forebode that wreck is nigh.

" Last night the gifted Seer did view
    A wet shroud swathed round ladye gay ;
Then stay thee, Fair, in Ravensheuch ;
    Why cross the gloomy firth to-day ? "—

" 'Tis not because Lord Lindesay's heir
    To-night at Roslin leads the ball,
But that my ladye-mother there
    Sits lonely in her castle-hall.

" 'Tis not because the ring they ride,
    And Lindesay at the ring rides well,
But that my sire the wine will chide,
    If 'tis not fill'd by Rosabelle."—

Inch = isle.

O'er Roslin all that dreary night,
  A wondrous blaze was seen to gleam ;
'Twas broader than the watch-fire's light,
  And redder than the bright moon-beam.

It glared on Roslin's castled rock,
  It ruddied all the copse-wood glen ;
'Twas seen from Dryden's groves of oak,
  And seen from cavern'd Hawthornden

Seem'd all on fire that chapel proud,
  Where Roslin's chiefs uncoffin'd lie ;
Each Baron, for a sable shroud,
  Sheathed in his iron panoply.

Seem'd all on fire within, around,
  Deep sacristy and altar's pale ;
Shone every pillar foliage-bound,
  And glimmer'd all the dead men's mail.

Blazed battlement and pinnet high,
  Blazed every rose-carved buttress fair—
So still they blaze, when fate is nigh
  The lordly line of high St. Clair.

There are twenty of Roslin's barons bold
  Lie buried within that proud chapelle ;
Each one the holy vault doth hold—
  But the sea holds lovely Rosabelle !

And each St. Clair was buried there,
  With candle, with book, and with knell ;
But the sea-caves rung, and the wild winds sung,
  The dirge of lovely Rosabelle !
                                SIR W. SCOTT.

THE PIPES AT LUCKNOW.

Pipes of the misty moorlands,
  Voice of the glens and hills;
The droning of the torrents,
  The treble of the rills!
Not the braes of broom and heather,
  Not the mountains dark with rain,
Nor maiden bower, nor border tower,
  Have heard your sweetest strain!

Dear to the Lowland reaper,
  And plaided mountaineer,—
To the cottage and the castle
  The Scottish pipes are dear;—
Sweet sounds the ancient pibroch
  O'er mountain, loch, and glade;
But the sweetest of all music
  The pipes at Lucknow played.

Day by day the Indian tiger
  Louder yelled, and nearer crept;
Round and round the jungle-serpent
  Near and nearer circles swept.
"Pray for rescue, wives and mothers,—
  Pray to-day!" the soldier said;
"To-morrow, death's between us
  And the wrong and shame we dread."

O, they listened, looked, and waited,
  Till their hope became despair;
And the sobs of low bewailing
  Filled the pauses of their prayer.

Then up spake a Scottish maiden,
  With her ear unto the ground :
" Dinna ye hear it ?—dinna ye hear it ?
  The pipes o' Havelock sound ! "

Hushed the wounded man his groaning ;
  Hushed the wife her little ones ;
Alone they heard the drum-roll
  And the roar of Sepoy guns.
But to sounds of home and childhood
  The Highland ear was true ;—
As the mother's cradle-crooning
  The mountain pipes she knew.

Like the march of soundless music
  Through the vision of the seer,
More of feeling than of hearing,
  Of the heart than of the ear,
She knew the droning pibroch,
  She knew the Campbell's call ;
" Hark ! hear ye no' Mac Gregor's,—
  The grandest o' them all ! "

O, they listened, dumb and breathless,
  And they caught the sound at last ;
Faint and far beyond the Goomtee,
  Rose and fell the piper's blast !
Then a burst of wild thanksgiving
  Mingled woman's voice and man's ;
" God be praised !—the march of Havelock !
  The piping of the clans ! "

Louder, nearer, fierce as vengeance,
  Sharp and shrill as swords at strife,
Came the wild Mac Gregor's clan-call,
  Stinging all the air to life.
But when the far-off dust-cloud
  To plaided legions grew,
Full tenderly and blithesomely
  The pipes of rescue blew !

Round the silver domes of Lucknow,
  Moslem mosque and Pagan shrine,
Breathed the air to Britons dearest,
  The air of Auld Lang Syne.
O'er the cruel roll of war-drums
  Rose that sweet and homelike strain ;
And the tartan clove the turban,
  As the Goomtee cleaves the plain.

Dear to the corn-land reaper
  And plaided mountaineer,—
To the cottage and the castle
  The piper's song is dear.
Sweet sounds the Gaelic pibroch
  O'er mountain, glen, and glade ;
But the sweetest of all music
  The Pipes at Lucknow played !

                              J. G. WHITTIER.

THE LADDER OF ST. AUGUSTINE.

SAINT AUGUSTINE ! well hast thou said,
  That of our vices we can frame
A ladder, if we will but tread
  Beneath our feet each deed of shame !

All common things, each day's events,
  That with the hour begin and end,
Our pleasures and our discontents,
  Are rounds by which we may ascend.

The low desire, the base design,
  That makes another's virtues less;
The revel of the ruddy wine,
  And all occasions of excess;

The longing for ignoble things;
  The strife for triumph more than truth;
The hardening of the heart, that brings
  Irreverence for the dreams of youth;

All thought of ill; all evil deeds,
  That have their root in thoughts of ill;
Whatever hinders or impedes
  The action of the nobler will;—

All these must first be trampled down
  Beneath our feet, if we would gain
In the bright fields of fair renown
  The right of eminent domain!

We have not wings, we cannot soar;
  But we have feet to scale and climb
By slow degrees, by more and more,
  The cloudy summits of our time.

The mighty pyramids of stone
  That wedge-like cleave the desert airs,
When nearer seen, and better known,
  Are but gigantic flights of stairs.

The distant mountains, that uprear
  Their solid bastions to the skies,
Are crossed by pathways, that appear
  As we to higher levels rise.

The heights by great men reached and kept,
  Were not attained by sudden flight,
But they, while their companions slept,
  Were toiling upward in the night.

Standing on what too long we bore
  With shoulders bent and downcast eyes,
We may discern, unseen before,
  A path to higher destinies.

Nor deem the irrevocable Past
  As wholly wasted, wholly vain,
If rising on its wrecks, at last,
  To something nobler we attain.

H. W. LONGFELLOW.

THE DIVERTING HISTORY OF JOHN GILPIN;

SHEWING HOW HE WENT FARTHER THAN HE INTENDED, AND
CAME SAFE HOME AGAIN.

JOHN GILPIN was a citizen
  Of credit and renown,
A trainband captain eke * was he
  Of famous London town.   -

John Gilpin's spouse said to her dear,
  " Though wedded we have been
These twice ten tedious years, yet we
  No holiday have seen.

" To-morrow is our wedding-day,
  And we will then repair
Unto the Bell at Edmonton
  All in a chaise and pair.

" My sister, and my sister's child,
  Myself, and children three,
Will fill the chaise; so you must ride
  On horseback after we."

* Eke = also.

He soon replied—"I do admire .
  Of womankind but one,
And you are she, my dearest dear,
  Therefore it shall be done.

" I am a linendraper bold,
  As all the world doth know,
And my good friend the calender
  Will lend his horse to go."

Quoth mistress Gilpin—"That's well said;
  And for that wine is dear,
We will be furnished with our own,
  Which is both bright and clear."

John Gilpin kiss'd his loving wife;
  O'erjoyed was he to find,
That, though on pleasure she was bent,
  She had a frugal mind.

The morning came, the chaise was brought,
  But yet was not allow'd
To drive up to the door, lest all
  Should say that she was proud.

So three doors off the chaise was stayed,
  Where they did all get in;
Six precious souls, and all agog
  To dash through thick and thin.

Smack went the whip, round went the wheels,
  Were never folk so glad,
The stones did rattle underneath,
  As if Cheapside were mad.

John Gilpin at his horse's side
  Seized fast the flowing mane,
And up he got, in haste to ride,
  But soon came down again;

For saddletree scarce reached had he,
, His journey to begin,
When, turning round his head, he saw
   Three customers come in.

So down he came; for loss of time,
   Although it grieved him sore,
Yet loss of pence, full well he knew,
   Would trouble him much more.

'Twas long before the customers
   Were suited to their mind,
When Betty screaming came down stairs—
   " The wine is left behind ! "

" Good lack ! " quoth he—" yet bring it me,
   My leathern belt likewise,
In which I bear my trusty sword
   When I do exercise."

Now mistress Gilpin (careful soul !)
   Had two stone bottles found,
To hold the liquor that she loved,
   And keep it safe and sound.

Each bottle had a curling ear,
   Through which the belt he drew,
And hung a bottle on each side,
   To make his balance true.

Then over all, that he might be
   Equipp'd from top to toe,
His long red cloak, well brush'd and neat,
   He manfully did throw.

Now see him mounted once again
   Upon his nimble steed,
Full slowly pacing o'er the stones,
   With caution and good heed.

K

But finding soon a smoother road
  Beneath his well shod feet,
The snorting beast began to trot,
  Which gall'd him in his seat.

So, "fair and softly," John he cried,
  But John he cried in vain ;
That trot became a gallop soon,
  In spite of curb and rein.

So stooping down, as needs he must
  Who cannot sit upright,
He grasp'd the mane with both his hands,
  And eke with all his might.

His horse, who never in that sort
  Had handled been before,
What thing upon his back had got
  Did wonder more and more.

Away went Gilpin, neck or naught ;
  Away went hat and wig ;
He little dreamt, when he set out,
  Of running such a rig.

The wind did blow, the cloak did fly,
  Like streamer long and gay,
Till, loop and button failing both,
  At last it flew away.

Then might all people well discern
  The bottles he had slung ;
A bottle swinging at each side,
  As hath been said or sung.

The dogs did bark, the children scream'd,
  Up flew the windows all ;
And every soul cried out, "Well done ! "
  As loud as he could bawl.

Away went Gilpin—who but he?
   His fame soon spread around;
"He carries weight!" "he rides a race!"
   "'Tis for a thousand pound!"

And still, as fast as he drew near,
   'Twas wonderful to view,
How in a trice the turnpike men
   Their gates wide open threw.

And now, as he went bowing down
   His reeking head full low,
The bottles twain behind his back
   Were shatter'd at a blow.

Down ran the wine into the road,
   Most piteous to be seen,
Which made his horse's flanks to smoke,
   As they had basted been.

But still he seem'd to carry weight,
   With leathern girdle braced;
For all might see the bottle necks
   Still dangling at his waist.

Thus all through merry Islington
   These gambols he did play,
Until he came unto the Wash
   Of Edmonton so gay;

And there he threw the Wash about
   On both sides of the way,
Just like unto a trundling mop,
   Or a wild goose at play.

At Edmonton, his loving wife
   From the balcony spied
Her tender husband, wondering much
   To see how he did ride.

" Stop, stop, John Gilpin !—Here's the house ; "
   They all at once did cry ;
" The dinner waits, and we are tired: "
   Said Gilpin—" So am I ! "

But yet his horse was not a whit
   Inclined to tarry there ;
For why ?—his owner had a house
   Full ten miles off, at Ware.

So like an arrow swift he flew,
   Shot by an archer strong ;
So did he fly—which brings me to
   The middle of my song.

Away went Gilpin, out of breath,
   And sore against his will,
Till, at his friend the calender's
   His horse at last stood still.

The calender, amazed to see
   His neighbour in such trim,
Laid down his pipe, flew to the gate,
   And thus accosted him :—

" What news ? what news ? your tidings tell ;
   Tell me you must and shall—
Say why bareheaded you are come,
   Or why you come at all ? "

Now Gilpin had a pleasant wit,
   And loved a timely joke ;
And thus unto the calender
   In merry guise, he spoke:

" I came because your horse would come ;
   And, if I well forbode,
My hat and wig will soon be here,—
   They are upon the road."

The calender, right glad to find
  His friend in merry pin,
Return'd him not a single word,
  But to the house went in ;

Whence straight he came with hat and wig ;
  A wig that flow'd behind,
A hat not much the worse for wear,
  Each comely in its kind.

He held them up, and in his turn
  Thus show'd his ready wit :
" My head is twice as big as yours,
  They therefore needs must fit.

" But let me scrape the dirt away
  That hangs upon your face ;
And stop and eat, for well you may
  Be in a hungry case."

Said John, " It is my wedding-day,
  And all the world would stare,
If wife should dine at Edmonton,
  And I should dine at Ware."

So turning to his horse, he said,
  " I am in haste to dine ;
'Twas for your pleasure you came here,
  You shall go back for mine."

Ah luckless speech, and bootless boast !
  For which he paid full dear ;
For, while he spake, a braying ass
  Did sing most loud and clear ;

Whereat his horse did snort, as he
  Had heard a lion roar,
And gallop'd off with all his might,
  As he had done before.

Away went Gilpin, and away
　　Went Gilpin's hat and wig :
He lost them sooner than at first,
　　For why ?—they were too big.

Now mistress Gilpin, when she saw
　　Her husband posting down
Into the country far away,
　　She pull'd out half-a-crown ;

And thus unto the youth she said,
　　That drove them to the Bell,
" This shall be yours, when you bring back
　　My husband safe and well."

The youth did ride, and soon did meet
　　John coming back amain ;
Whom in a trice he tried to stop,
　　By catching at his rein ;

But, not performing what he meant,
　　And gladly would have done,
The frighted steed he frighted more,
　　And made him faster run.

Away went Gilpin, and away
　　Went postboy at his heels,
The postboy's horse right glad to miss
　　The lumbering of the wheels.

Six gentlemen upon the road
　　Thus seeing Gilpin fly,
With postboy scampering in the rear,
　　They raised the hue and cry :—

" Stop thief ! stop thief !—a highwayman !"
　　Not one of them was mute ;
And all and each that pass'd that way
　　Did join in the pursuit.

And now the turnpike-gates again
  Flew open in short space;
The toll-men thinking as before,
  That Gilpin rode a race.

And so he did, and won it too,
  For he got first to town;
Nor stopp'd till where he had got up
  He did again get down.

Now let us sing, long live the king,
  And Gilpin, long live he;
And when he next doth ride abroad,
  May I be there to see!

                              W. COWPER.

THE BALLAD OF CHEVY CHASE.

GOD prosper long our noble king,
  Our lives and safeties all;
A woful hunting once there did
  In Chevy Chase befall.

To drive the deer with hound and horn
  Earl Percy took his way;
The child may rue that is unborn
  The hunting of that day.

The stout Earl of Northumberland
  A vow to God did make,
His pleasure in the Scottish woods
  Three summer days to take;

The chiefest harts in Chevy Chase
  To kill and bear away:
These tidings to Earl Douglas came
  In Scotland, where he lay;

Who sent Earl Percy present word,
　He would prevent his sport;
The English earl, not fearing that,
　Did to the woods resort,

With fifteen hundred bowmen bold,
　All chosen men of might,
Who knew full well in time of need,
　To aim their shafts aright.

The gallant greyhounds swiftly ran,
　To chase the fallow deer;
On Monday they began to hunt,
　When daylight did appear;

And, long before high noon they had
　A hundred fat bucks slain;
Then, having dined, the drovers went
　To rouse the deer again.

Lord Percy to the quarry went,
　To view the slaughter'd deer;
Quoth he, "Earl Douglas promised
　This day to meet me here;

"But if I thought he would not come,
　No longer would I stay."
With that a brave young gentleman
　Thus to the earl did say:

*Lo, yonder doth Earl Douglas come,
　His men in armour bright;
Full twenty hundred Scottish spears
　All marching in our sight.

"All men of pleasant Tividale,
　Fast by the river Tweed."
*"Then cease your sport," Earl Percy said,
　"And take your bows with speed:

" And now with me, my countrymen,
    Your courage forth advance ;
For never was there champion yet
    In Scotland or in France,

" That ever did on horseback come,
    But, if my hap it were,
I durst encounter, man for man,
    With him to break a spear."

Earl Douglas, on a milk-white steed,
    Most like a baron bold,
Rode foremost of the company,
    Whose armour shone like gold.

" Show me," said he, " whose men you be
    That hunt so boldly here,
That, without my consent, do chase
    And kill my fallow deer."

The man that first did answer make
    Was noble Percy, he ;
Who said, " We list not to declare,
    Nor show whose men we be :

" Yet will we spend our dearest blood
    The chiefest harts to slay ; "
Then Douglas made a solemn oath,
    And thus in rage did say ;

" Ere thus I will out-braved be
    One of us two shall die :
I know thee well, an earl thou art ;
    Lord Percy : so am I.

" But, trust me, Percy, pity it were,
    And great offence, to kill
Any of these our guiltless men,
    For they have done no ill.

" Let thou and I the battle try,
    And set our men aside."
" Accurst be he," Lord Percy said,
    " By whom this is denied."

Then stepp'd a gallant squire forth,
    Witherington was his name,
Who said, " I would not have it told
    To Henry our king, for shame,

" That e'er my captain fought on foot
    And I stood looking on :
Ye be two earls," said Witherington,
    " And I a squire alone.

" I'll do my best that do I may,
    While I have strength to stand ;
While I have power to wield my sword,
    I'll fight with heart and hand."

Our English archers bent their bows,
    Their hearts were good and true ;
At the first flight of arrows sent,
    Full fourscore Scots they slew.

They closed full fast on ev'ry side,
    No slackness was there found ;
And many a gallant gentleman
    Lay gasping on the ground.

In sooth it was a grief to see,
    And likewise for to hear,
The cries of men lying in their gore,
    And scatter'd here and there.

At last these two stout earls did meet,
    Like captains of great might ;
.Like lions moved, they laid on load,
    And made a cruel fight.

"Yield thee, Lord Percy," Douglas said;
  "In faith I will thee bring,
Where thou shalt high advanced be,
  By James our Scottish King.

"Thy ransom I will freely give,
  And thus report of thee:
Thou art the most courageous knight
  That ever I did see."

"No, Douglas," quoth Lord Percy then,
  "Thy proffer I do scorn;
I will not yield to any Scot
  That ever yet was born."

With that there came an arrow keen
  Out of an English bow,
Which struck Earl Douglas to the heart,
  A deep and deadly blow:

Who never spoke more words than these,
  "Fight on, my merry men all!
For why, my life is at an end:
  Lord Percy sees my fall."

Then leaving life, Earl Percy took
  The dead man by the hand;
And said, "Earl Douglas, for thy life
  Would I had lost my land!

A Knight amongst the Scots there was,
  Which saw Earl Douglas die,
Who straight in wrath did vow revenge
  Upon the Earl Percy:

Sir Hugh Montgomery was he call'd,
  Who, with a spear most bright,
Well mounted on a gallant steed,
  Ran fiercely through the fight;

And pass'd the English archers all,
  Without all dread or fear,
And through Earl Percy's body then
  He thrust his hateful spear:

So thus did both these nobles die,
  Whose courage none could stain;
An English archer then perceiv'd
  The noble Earl was slain:

He had a bow bent in his hand,
  Made of a trusty tree;
An arrow of a cloth-yard long
  Up to the head drew he.

Against Sir Hugh Montgomery
  So right the shaft he set,
The grey-goose wing that was thereon
  In his heart's blood was wet.

This fight did last from break of day
  Till setting of the sun;
For when they rang the evening-bell,
  The battle scarce was done.

Of fifteen hundred Englishmen
  Went home but fifty-three;
The rest were slain in Chevy Chase,
  Under the greenwood tree.

Next day did many widows come,
  Their husbands to bewail;
They washed their wounds in brinish tears,
  But all would not prevail.

Their bodies, bath'd in purple blood,
  They bore with them away;
They kiss'd them dead a thousand times
  Ere they were clad in clay.

This news was brought to Edinburgh,
   Where Scotland's king did reign,
'That brave Earl Douglas, suddenly
   Was with an arrow slain.

" Oh heavy news ! " King James did say ;
   " Scotland can witness be,
I have not any captain more
   Of such account as he."

Like tidings to King Henry came,
   Within as short a space,
That Percy, of Northumberland,
   Was slain in Chevy Chase.

" Now God be with him," said our King,
   " Sith't will no better be ;
I trust I have within my realm
   Five hundred good as he."

God save the King, and bless this land
   In plenty, joy, and peace ;
And grant henceforth, that foul debate
   'Twixt noblemen may cease !

THE DREAM OF EUGENE ARAM.

'Twas in the prime of summer time,
   An evening calm and cool,
And four-and-twenty happy boys
   Came bounding out of school :
There were some that ran, and some that leapt,
   Like troutlets in a pool.

Away they sped with gamesome minds,
   And souls untouch'd by sin ;
To a level mead they came, and there
   They drave the wickets in :
Pleasantly shone the setting sun
   Over the town of Lynn.

Like sportive deer they coursed about,
   And shouted as they ran,—
Turning to mirth all things of earth,
   As only boyhood can;
But the Usher sat remote from all,
   A melancholy man!

His hat was off, his vest apart,
   To catch heaven's blessed breeze;
For a burning thought was in his brow,
   And his bosom ill at ease:
So he lean'd his head on his hands, and read
   The book between his knees!

Leaf after leaf he turn'd it o'er,
   Nor ever glanced aside,
For the peace of his soul he read that book
   In the golden eventide:
Much study had made him very lean,
   And pale, and leaden-eyed.

At last he shut the ponderous tome,
   With a fast and fervent grasp
He strain'd the dusky covers close,
   And fix'd the brazen hasp:
"Oh, God! could I so close my mind,
   And clasp it with a clasp!"

Then leaping on his feet upright,
   Some moody turns he took,—
Now up the mead, then down the mead,
   And past a shady nook.—
And lo! he saw a little boy
   That pored upon a book!

"My gentle lad, what is't you read—
   Romance or fairy fable?
Or is it some historic page,
   Of kings and crowns unstable?"
The young boy gave an upward glance,—
   "It is 'The Death of Abel.'"

The Usher took six hasty strides,
  As smit with sudden pain,—
Six hasty strides beyond the place,
  Then slowly back again;
And down he sat beside the lad,
  And talk'd with him of Cain;

And, long since then, of bloody men,
  Whose deeds tradition saves;
Of lonely folk cut off unseen,
  And hid in sudden graves;
Of horrid stabs, in groves forlorn,
  And murders done in caves;

And how the sprites of injured men
  Shriek upward from the sod,—
Aye, how the ghostly hand will point
  To show the burial clod;
And unknown facts of guilty acts
  Are seen in dreams from God!

He told how murderers walk the earth
  Beneath the curse of Cain,—
With crimson clouds before their eyes,
  And flames about their brain:
For blood has left upon their souls
  Its everlasting stain!

" And well," quoth he, " I know, for truth,
  Their pangs must be extreme,—
Woe, woe, unutterable woe,—
  Who spill life's sacred stream!
For why? Methought, last night, I wrought
  A murder, in a dream!

"One that had never done me wrong—
  A feeble man, and old;
I led him to a lonely field,—
  The moon shone clear and cold:
Now here, said I, this man shall die,
  And I will have his gold!

" Two sudden blows with a ragged stick,
   And one with a heavy stone,
One hurried gash with a hasty knife,—
   And then the deed was done:
There was nothing lying at my foot,
   But lifeless flesh and bone!

" Nothing but lifeless flesh and bone,
   That could not do me ill;
And yet I fear'd him all the more
   For lying there so still:
There was a manhood in his look,
   That murder could not kill!

" And lo! the universal air
   Seem'd lit with ghastly flame;—
Ten thousand thousand dreadful eyes
   Were looking down in blame:
I took the dead man by the hand,
   And call'd upon his name!

" Oh God! it made me quake to see
   Such sense within the slain!
But when I touched the lifeless clay,
   The blood gush'd out amain!
For every clot, a burning spot
   Was scorching in my brain!

" My head was like an ardent coal,
   My heart as solid ice;
My wretched, wretched soul, I knew,
   Was at the Devil's price:
A dozen times I groan'd; the dead
   Had never groan'd but twice!

" And now from forth the frowning sky,
   From the Heaven's topmost height,
I heard a voice—the awful voice
   Of the blood-avenging Sprite:—
' Thou guilty man! take up thy dead
   And hide it from my sight!'

"I took the dreary body up,
    And cast it in a stream,—
A sluggish water, black as ink,
    The depth was so extreme :—
My gentle Boy, remember this
    Is nothing but a dream !

"Down went the corse with a hollow plunge,
    And vanish'd in the pool;
Anon I cleansed my bloody hands,
    And wash'd my forehead cool,
And sat among the urchins young,
    That evening in the school.

"Oh, Heaven ! to think of their white souls,
    And mine so black and grim !
I could not share in childish prayer,
    Nor join in Evening Hymn :
Like a Devil of the Pit I seem'd,
    'Mid holy Cherubim !

"And peace went with them, one and all,
    And each calm pillow spread ;
But Guilt was my grim Chamberlain
    That lighted me to bed ;
And drew my midnight curtains round,
    With fingers bloody red !

"All night I lay in agony,
    In anguish dark and deep ;
My fever'd eyes I dared not close,
    But stared aghast at Sleep :
For Sin had render'd unto her
    The keys of Hell to keep !

"All night I lay in agony,
    From weary chime to chime,
With one besetting horrid hint,
    That rack'd me all the time ;
A mighty yearning, like the first
    Fierce impulse unto crime !

L

" One stern tyrannic thought, that made
　All other thoughts its slave ;
Stronger and stronger every pulse
　Did that temptation crave,—
Still urging me to go and see
　The Dead Man in his grave !

" Heavily I rose up, as soon
　As light was in the sky,
And sought the black accursed pool
　With a wild misgiving eye ;
And I saw the Dead in the river bed,
　For the faithless stream was dry.

" Merrily rose the lark, and shook
　The dewdrop from its wing ;
But I never mark'd its morning flight,
　I never heard it sing :
For I was stooping once again
　Under the horrid thing.

" With breathless speed, like a soul in chase,
　I took him up and ran ;—
There was no time to dig a grave
　Before the day began :
In a lonesome wood, with heaps of leaves,
　I hid the murdered man !

" And all that day I read in school,
　But my thought was other where ;
As soon as the mid-day task was done,
　In secret I was there :
And a mighty wind had swept the leaves,
　And still the corse was bare !

" Then down I cast me on my face,
　And first began to weep,
For I knew my secret then was one
　That earth refused to keep :
Or land or sea, though he should be
　Ten thousand fathoms deep.

" So wills the fierce avenging Sprite,
  Till blood for blood atones !
Ay, though he's buried in a cave,
  And trodden down with stones,
And years have rotted off his flesh,—
  The world shall see his bones !

" Oh, God ! that horrid, horrid dream
  Besets me now awake !
Again—again, with dizzy brain,
  The human life I take;
And my red right hand grows raging hot,
  Like Cranmer's at the stake.

" And still no peace for the restless clay
  Will wave or mould allow;
The horrid thing pursues my soul,—
  It stands before me now ! "
The fearful Boy look'd up, and saw
  Huge drops upon his brow !

That very night, while gentle sleep
  The urchin eyelids kiss'd,
Two stern-faced men set out from Lynn,
  Through the cold and heavy mist;
And Eugene Aram walk'd between,
  With gyves upon his wrist.
             T. Hood.

MY LOST YOUTH.

Often I think of the beautiful town,
  That is seated by the sea;
Often in thought go up and down
The pleasant streets of that dear old town,
  And my youth comes back to me.
      And a verse of a Lapland song
      Is haunting my memory still:
   " A boy's will is the wind's will,
And the thoughts of youth are long, long thoughts."

I can see the shadowy lines of its trees,
    And catch, in sudden gleams,
The sheen of the far-surrounding seas,
And islands that were the Hesperides
    Of all my boyish dreams.
        And the burden of that old song,
        It murmurs and whispers still:
    "A boy's will is the wind's will,
And the thoughts of youth are long, long thoughts."

I remember the black wharves and the slips,
    And the sea-tides tossing free;
And Spanish sailors with bearded lips,
And the beauty and mystery of the ships,
    And the magic of the sea.
        And the voice of that wayward song
        Is singing and saying still:
    "A boy's will is the wind's will,
And the thoughts of youth are long, long thoughts."

I remember the bulwarks by the shore,
    And the fort upon the hill;
The sunrise gun, with its hollow roar,
The drum-beat repeated o'er and o'er,
    And the bugle wild and shrill.
        And the music of that old song
        Throbs in my memory still:
    "A boy's will is the wind's will,
And the thoughts of youth are long, long thoughts."

I remember the sea-fight far away,
    How it thundered o'er the tide!
And the dead captains, as they lay
In their graves, o'erlooking the tranquil bay,
    Where they in battle died.
        And the sound of that mournful song
        Goes through me with a thrill:
    "A boy's will is the wind's will,
And the thoughts of youth are long, long thoughts."

I can see the breezy dome of groves,
    The shadows of Deering's Woods;
And the friendships old and the early loves
Come back with a sabbath sound, as of doves
    In quiet neighbourhoods.
        And the verse of that sweet old song,
        It flutters and murmurs still:
    " A boy's will is the wind's will,
And the thoughts of youth are long, long thoughts."

I remember the gleams and glooms that dart
    Across the school-boy's brain;
The song and the silence in the heart,
That in part are prophecies, and in part
    Are longings wild and vain.
        And the voice of that fitful song
        Sings on, and is never still:
    " A boy's will is the wind's will,
And the thoughts of youth are long, long thoughts."

There are things of which I may not speak;
    There are dreams that cannot die;
There are thoughts that make the strong heart weak,
And bring a pallor into the cheek,
    And a mist before the eye.
        And the words of that fatal song
        Come over me like a chill:
    " A boy's will is the wind's will,
And the thoughts of youth are long, long thoughts."

Strange to me now are the forms I meet
    When I visit the dear old town;
But the native air is pure and sweet,
And the trees that o'ershadow each well-known street,
    As they balance up and down,
        Are singing the beautiful song,
        Are sighing and whispering still:
    " A boy's will is the wind's will,
And the thoughts of youth are long, long thoughts."

And Deering's Woods are fresh and fair,
    And with joy that is almost pain
My heart goes back to wander there,
And among the dreams of the days that were,
    I find my lost youth again.
      And the strange and beautiful song,
      The groves are repeating it still:
    " A boy's will is the wind's will,
And the thoughts of youth are long, long thoughts.'
           H. W. LONGFELLOW.

THE END.

LONDON: PRINTED BY WILLIAM CLOWES AND SONS, LIMITED,
STAMFORD STREET AND CHARING CROSS.

www.ingramcontent.com/pod-product-compliance
Lightning Source LLC
Chambersburg PA
CBHW021127020726
47500CB00003B/953